A LADY TO LEAD

A LADY TO LEAD

SISTERS
of the
REVOLUTION #2

Audrey Glenn

DAUGHTERS OF COLUMBIA BOOKS

First printing, 2020

Published by Daughters of Columbia Books

ISBN 978-1-940096-42-1

PRINTED IN THE UNITED STATES OF AMERICA

—For Cliff
This is a business trip!

Chapter 1

Helen Crofton stood in front of the looking glass in her small bedroom and nervously readjusted her tan and floral jacket for the third time. The jacket was fine—it was Helen that was discomfited. In another hour, her sister Cassandra would nominate her as president of the Philadelphia Young Ladies Charitable Society, and the group could finally do some good. Or something at all. *If* the other young ladies accepted her, that was. At least Helen's dark hair looked well—powdered and curled in the latest fashion.

She smiled into the glass, attempting to cultivate an expression simultaneously confident and friendly. One that would inspire trust. She relaxed her face until her lips were turned up a moderate amount and inclined her head forward a touch. That was the one—pleasant and poised. She couldn't know if her smile would have the intended effect on the charitable society, but it would have to do.

Helen left her bedroom and followed her brother-in-law's voice down the corridor of their shared apartment to the drawing room, recently repainted in the gray-blue color he favored.

David Beaufort stood back to admire the lines on his latest acquisition. "What a remarkably elegant chair."

"Was it worth the time you spent deliberating, dearest?" Cassandra teased. The sisters had been subjected to David's agonizing for weeks.

"Don't you think so? You can sit turned any way you like." He sat to demonstrate, pivoting from right to left while leaning against each side of the backrest in turn. "Perfect for parties. I can speak to your aunt and then turn to your uncle with no discomfort at all!"

"Hmm." Cassandra massaged her lower back.

"Oh—you should sit, my love." David sprang from the seat and beckoned to his pregnant wife to take his place, helping her into the chair.

"Are you ready?" Helen interrupted, stepping farther into the drawing room.

David whirled around. "Ah, Helen! You should have a turn also."

No matter how trivial Helen found his obsession with furniture, David's delight was infectious, and Helen smiled back. "It's a lovely chair," she conceded. "Perhaps I can try it later."

Cassandra glanced at the clock on the mantel. "Do you want to go now?"

"I don't want to risk being late."

"Let me send Westing down to the stables to order our coach." David started for the door immediately.

"No need," Cassandra called out before he made it out of the room. "We can walk down and order the coach ourselves."

"Westing doesn't mind going." David turned back. "He could use the fresh air."

"As can we." Cassandra started to use the arm of the new

2

chair to stand, but David dashed back to help her the rest of the way to her feet.

He touched his forehead to Cassandra's, never able to resist an opportunity to caress his wife. "Don't forget to order the coach. It's a long walk to your aunt and uncle's home, and I don't want anything to happen to you or the baby."

Cassandra gently patted his cheek. "We'll be perfectly safe for the entire mile, I assure you! Now, what will you do while we're gone?"

"Visit the coffee room at City Tavern and then collect Nathaniel for dinner."

That caught Helen's attention. "Captain Carter! Is he to dine with us?"

Cassandra's smile grew a touch fixed as she replied. "I told David he could invite a friend."

"I thought Captain Carter was a business associate." Helen kept her tone pleasant despite the disagreeable surprise.

"I like him, and it *is* my birthday," David pointed out.

Helen adopted her lately practiced smile. "True, but couldn't you think of anyone else in Philadelphia to invite? Dr. Rush, perhaps."

David opened his mouth to respond, probably something about how Helen didn't care for Dr. Rush either, but Cassandra used one finger to lift his chin, then stood on tiptoes to kiss him. Helen glanced away for decency's sake, though in truth, one had to quash any inclination to condemn public displays of affection when one lived with a pair so enamored of each other.

"Are you sure you don't want me to escort you?" David asked, and Helen knew it was safe to look again.

"Certainly not. Enjoy the coffee room. And your new chair."

"Be careful, please, dearest." David kissed Cassandra's hand then looked to Helen. "Good luck today."

"Oh—thank you." It was thoughtful of David to remember the election, but luck would be irrelevant if they were late.

"Come," Cassandra said. Fastening their cloaks, they made their way down the narrow stairs from the second-floor apartment over their uncle's law office. Helen didn't see Uncle Josiah among his clerks to bid him goodbye. Perhaps he was in his private study or arguing a case in court.

The ladies began for their aunt and uncle's home in the chilly October air. Helen paused in front of the stable that housed David's coach and horses, but Cassandra walked past without stopping. "Didn't you tell David we would ask for the coach?"

"I told him we *could* order it. I didn't say we *would*."

Helen stepped over a pile of horse droppings as she followed her sister. "Very clever misdirection." Cassandra was determined not to be wrapped away in linen until after the baby came.

"You needn't race there," Cassandra chided. "We're quite early."

"I'm sorry. I just don't want to be late." Helen forced herself to walk at what felt like a snail's pace.

"All will be well," Cassandra assured her. "I'll nominate you as president, and I'm certain Patience or Constance will second it."

Helen couldn't stop herself from voicing concerns they'd covered a dozen times already. "But will they vote for me, or will they all wish to see Temperance reelected instead?"

Cassandra looped her arm through Helen's. "I doubt Temperance wants to be president again. She seemed to lose interest very quickly."

"You're too polite to say we accomplished nothing during her tenure," Helen muttered. She'd arrived at each meeting seeking worthwhile projects to complete, but Temperance wasted every minute talking of balls and beaus.

"Spending an hour in conversation with our friends is not completely wasted time," her sister pointed out.

"*Your* friends. I don't think any of them truly like me." How could they? In her previous life in England, Helen had been appreciated for her good sense and capable management, but she hadn't had the opportunity to demonstrate those things in Philadelphia.

Cassandra shook her head. "We've talked about this. They *do* like you."

"Then why did no one support my suggestions? I recommended we hold a subscription ball to raise money for a statue of William Penn—"

"—which Patience rightly pointed out would not be sufficiently profitable," Cassandra interrupted.

Even Helen had to concede when Patience had done the sums comparing what they could reasonably charge for admission against the cost of renting the rooms and serving refreshments, but that hadn't been her only suggestion. "I also proposed that we beautify the grounds surrounding the potter's field in Southeast Square."

Cassandra frowned in mock concentration. "If I remember correctly, even you didn't relish the thought of digging about in the dirt."

Also true. Helen needed better ideas to present. "Be that as it may, if I'm elected president, we'll do *something*."

"Will you allow me to make a suggestion?"

Helen nodded.

"Involve the other ladies in planning and accomplishing the charitable work. You don't have to do things alone."

"I always welcome other people's assistance," Helen

assured Cassandra. She caught her sister trying to hide a laugh. "I do! I only take on what no one else wishes to." Besides, the other ladies could hardly see her as someone worthy of respect if she sat back and forced them to do everything.

"If you say so."

Despite Cassandra's leisurely walking speed, they arrived at the Hayeses' brick home plenty early for the meeting. Ginny, one of the maids, answered the door.

Helen handed over her cloak. "How is your mother?"

"Dr. Drinker's been by to see her. Says her heart is weak." Ginny shook her head sadly.

Cassandra laid a hand on Ginny's arm before handing over her own cloak. "Oh dear, perhaps we can visit her soon."

"Thank you; she would like that." Ginny smiled gratefully before directing them to the drawing room.

Helen cast a significant look at her sister, but Cassandra blushed and wouldn't meet her eyes. Dr. Drinker had been very pointed in his attentions to Cassandra before she married David. She always insisted the relationship was strictly professional, and while Helen had no doubt that was true on her sister's side, she couldn't pass up the opportunity to tease her.

Their cousin Patience Hayes sat at a table in the elegant, green-paneled drawing room, scribbling away. She glanced up when they walked in and smiled politely before returning to her work. "Is it time already? Temperance should be down soon. I have to finish this volume of Virginia legal cases for Papa's trial. I've managed to find one instance where a general court prevented a magistrate from setting aside a jury's verdict, but I'd like to find a few more."

"Your father is very fortunate to have your assistance." Helen took a seat on the couch next to Patience.

Patience shook her head wryly. "With no sons, he has no other options. His apprentice is overworked as it is, and his current crop of clerks don't have much promise."

"You would be an asset if he had half a dozen sons." As a child, Helen had often sat in her own father's lap while he spoke to his steward, and sometimes he would ask her opinion about what he should do. How adult and respected he'd made her feel! Patience was blessed to have a father who trusted her to do research for him.

Jane Allen arrived next, dressed in a simple gray gown befitting her Quaker faith. She nodded to the room and quietly took her seat.

Helen's stomach churned. Not much longer now, and she'd find out if she would be in a position to make changes in the society.

Temperance Hayes glided into the drawing room, her sister Constance trailing behind. "Are we all here?" Temperance took a chair prominently placed near the fire. "I have something to say to you all."

Before she could explain, Euphemia Goodwin burst into the room. "I'm ever so sorry; my dancing master kept me so long! Am I late?"

"Not at all," Helen reassured Euphemia. Euphemia offered a grateful smile and dashed for the last open seat. Helen forced her hands to rest still on her lap. Did Temperance's announcement have anything to do with her position as the society's president?

Temperance waited for Euphemia to settle herself before beginning again. "Put that book away, Constance; I don't wish for you to miss what I have to say." Constance dutifully stuffed a novel behind her back and looked expectantly towards Temperance. "I want you all to know that I shan't run for re-election as president. I'll be unable to devote the time required, as I shall soon enter a different sphere of life."

Patience's lips tightened at her sister's words, but Euphemia sat forward, eyes wide. "Whatever do you mean?"

Temperance toyed with one of the locks of hair draped elegantly over her shoulder. "I can say no more. Nothing is yet official."

"She plans to be married," Constance whispered loudly.

Euphemia squealed and clapped. "How wonderful! Who is the man?"

"As I said, nothing is official, and it would be extremely improper of me to say more. I just wanted all of you to know that the *only* thing that could prevent me from carrying on with the noble work of this society is an even higher calling. I'm certain I can trust each of you not to spread this about before it's settled." Temperance sat back in her chair and folded her hands in her lap like royalty.

Helen and Cassandra exchanged a look. Temperance must have finally captured Winthrop Morley's attentions. She'd been angling to marry the governor's worthless scoundrel of a son for as long as the sisters had known her.

"With that critical announcement, should we call for nominations for a new president?" Patience's sarcastic tone made it clear she found Temperance's proclamation anything but important.

Cassandra spoke up quickly. "I nominate Helen."

Helen adopted her practiced smile and surreptitiously observed the other ladies' reactions. Jane was grave as always, while Constance nodded slowly. Temperance seemed surprised, but Patience smiled approvingly.

"How wonderful!" Euphemia declared. "I second the nomination!"

Helen beamed at her. She hadn't expected support from that quarter, but she vowed she would never again be annoyed with Euphemia's prattle.

"Anyone else?" Patience asked. Helen reminded herself to breathe.

No one suggested another name.

"All in favor?"

Every hand rose. Helen looked around the room at the other ladies, and her heart swelled. They wished her to be their president. She'd spare no effort to prove their trust was not in vain.

"Very good; the 'ayes' have it. Helen, you are our new president." Patience recorded the change of leadership in her minutes.

Helen stood hastily and tried to recall what she'd planned to say if actually elected. "Thank you for your trust in me. I hope I shall honor this society by my efforts. I'd especially like to choose a charitable project we could begin immediately."

Euphemia hung off her chair and frantically waved one hand in the air, dainty mouth pursed with excitement. Helen nodded for Euphemia to share her suggestion. "I just know you'll do an admirable job, Helen, and I'm delighted to join all of you in this righteous endeavor. I think there's a great deal wrong with this city that we young ladies can set to rights, for it's not just the gentlemen of Philadelphia who are able to enact reforms. In fact, I was just saying to my father—"

Euphemia would likely go on for a quarter of an hour if Helen didn't intercede. "Thank you, Euphemia. Perhaps you can tell us what you said to your father after the meeting? I don't wish for us to run out of time to discuss our ideas."

Euphemia threw her hands over her face. "I'm sorry," she apologized, her words muffled through her fingers.

"Think nothing of it." Helen smiled politely at her. "Are there any ideas for projects?"

"We could knit caps for the poor," Constance suggested. "It must be very troublesome to be poor when it is this cold."

Helen didn't want to admit that neither she nor her sister could knit in front of the accomplished Hayes sisters. "That's certainly one idea. Any others?"

Jane raised a hand. "I've become aware of a young girl, just fifteen, who arrived from England in the spring. She has become the recipient of some very improper attentions from her master's son, which have made her very unhappy, but her contract is in force for six more years."

Helen's breath caught. She'd very nearly been sold into indenture with her sister when they'd first arrived in Philadelphia.

"I feel for her most intensely!" Temperance declared. "This must be our project."

Though she agreed with Temperance, Helen couldn't help feeling a little irritated that her cousin was inserting herself into the decision. She'd let the other ladies make the final verdict. "Shall we put it to a vote?" All hands went in the air.

Patience tapped her fingers on her lap. "How can we raise money for the contract? Indentures for a young person can cost as much as twenty-five pounds."

"I know!" Euphemia stuck one finger in the air. "I'll ask my father to give us the money."

That notion didn't sit well with Helen. "It won't be truly our work if we ask the men in our lives to pay for it." Most of the ladies nodded, though Temperance raised a skeptical brow.

Euphemia jumped up from her seat, startling Helen. "Oh!

We might each sell our hair! My maid told me that a really fine head might garner five pounds, and there are seven of us here—we might almost free two servants!"

Helen wasn't the only lady to spontaneously raise a hand to her head. "Um, very admirable sentiment, Euphemia. Any other ideas?"

Jane raised her hand for the second time. "We could sell a baked good in High Street Market."

Helen brightened. "That's a wonderful idea! Our father used to host a fête every year to benefit our poorest tenants, and Cassandra and I always contributed to the baked goods sale." Memories of a happier time deluged her mind. She hadn't fully appreciated how wonderful her life had been until her parents died and everything changed.

Euphemia clapped with excitement. "We should make a syllabub. I love syllabub above all things!"

"That might be very difficult, Euphemia," Cassandra pointed out. "A syllabub must be consumed just when it is made, and one could not prepare very many at once."

"Gooseberry tarts!" The words burst from Helen's mouth. "They were always very popular at the fêtes."

Patience frowned. "Gooseberries aren't in season."

"We can use gooseberry preserves," Helen countered. Gooseberry tarts would certainly prove just as profitable to sell in Philadelphia as they had at Heartcomb.

Jane wasn't finished with her suggestions. "I thought we might serve gingerbread. It's easy to cut and stays fresh for several days when wrapped."

"We dined on gooseberry tart at the governor's house last summer," Helen pointed out. "And Mrs. Morley was very fashionable and elite." She'd passed away the following autumn, poor lady, but her death was from illness and nothing to do with the desserts she'd served. It was practically honoring her memory to serve gooseberry tarts.

Jane nodded, though the set to her lips made her appear less than convinced.

"It's settled then," Helen announced. "I'll draw up a plan for the entire scheme, and we'll discuss it at our next meeting. This meeting is adjourned."

After visiting a little while, the sisters took their leave. The day was crisp and clear, and the last of the autumn leaves provided a lovely frame for the beautiful red-brick city.

Helen slid her arm through her sister's. "I love this city in the fall!"

"Does it seem lovelier to you now that you've been elected president?" Cassandra teased. "I take it you were pleased with the meeting."

"Yes, I think it went very well. That young girl we are to help—that could have easily been you and me."

Cassandra shook her head. "Thank heaven for our uncle!"

"I can't wait to make the gooseberry tarts. It will feel like we're home again." Helen's mouth watered. She could almost taste the tart berries.

"Are you certain you know how to make them? As I recall, we didn't really do much more than watch Cook prepare the tarts."

As if Helen could ever forget such a happy time in her life. "I remember every detail, and I've Mama's household book to refer to."

"Receipts are often more difficult to execute than to read," Cassandra insisted. "Perhaps Peggy could help you."

Helen patted her sister's hand. "I'm certain I can manage,

but it's comforting to know we have an expert cook around to ask questions of."

"I wonder what Peggy's preparing for David's birthday dinner." Cassandra smiled with anticipation.

That put Helen in mind of the guest list. "While we're on the subject, why didn't you tell me Captain Carter was coming?"

Cassandra cast her eyes to the sky. "Perhaps I didn't wish to hear you complain of it for days."

"I wouldn't have! I would have appreciated the chance to prepare myself to receive him with equanimity. Do you not recall how rude he was to me at your wedding? First, he ignored me, then he laid hands upon my person—"

"To try to save your life, if I remember," her sister interjected.

"—refused to laugh about the whole thing and treated me like a spectacle at a village fair," Helen finished. Cassandra's lips twitched, but she didn't say anything.

Helen was only warming up to the subject. "I *always* attempt to make conversation with him when his company is forced upon me. The last time I saw him, I asked him about his new ship, and he answered in three words. Then he turned to David and spoke at length of the Pennsylvania silk industry."

"An excessively boring discussion," Cassandra had to own. "One would hardly guess he'd be such a poor conversationalist."

Helen nodded vigorously. "I've often thought it a pity his manners aren't as pleasing as his outward appearance."

Cassandra gave Helen a sideways glance. "I only meant it's surprising that a well-traveled and successful businessman can't seem to hold a conversation with you. I'd no idea you esteemed his appearance so highly."

Helen looked forward, but she could still feel Cassandra's gaze on her. Why had she let such an embarrassing observation slip out? "I'm not so prejudiced against the man that I can't admit he's handsome."

His good looks were the first thing she'd noticed about him when they met at David and Cassandra's wedding celebration, but any hope Captain Carter would prove a prospective suitor had been dashed to pieces nearly as soon as he'd opened his mouth.

Cassandra continued to openly scrutinize Helen. "I must confess that this puts your dislike of him in an entirely new light."

Helen sniffed. "I suppose you think I only loathe him because I feel spurned, or some such."

"Yes, that's precisely what I think." Cassandra gasped.

Helen stopped in the street. "What's wrong? Is it the baby?"

Cassandra shook Helen's arm a little in excitement. "Perhaps you make Captain Carter nervous because he's also enamored of you!"

Helen sighed heavily and pulled her sister forward. "Don't be ridiculous. He's made no secret of how inadequate he finds me." He'd scorned her clothing and looked with horror at her tears over a prospective parting from her sister. "And I'm not enamored of him, so I don't know why you'd imply that I share such a sentiment even if it wasn't fantastical to think Captain Carter is capable of such an attitude."

Cassandra gave Helen a very pointed look. "Well, it won't hurt you to try to be pleasant to him tonight, for David's sake, if not for your own."

"Very well, but only for David." Helen imagined greeting the man warmly and him complimenting the new silk gown David insisted on purchasing for her, then shook her head. It would never happen.

She'd try being friendly at dinner, but when that failed, she'd show him how little she depended on his notice. She had much more important things to worry about than obstinate sea captains, in any event. As early as she could politely manage, she would escape to her bedroom and begin working on the plan for the society.

Chapter 2

Nathaniel Carter groaned and threw a crumpled note across the room. Such terrible news was the last thing he needed.

"Hold!"

Nathaniel looked up to see David Beaufort, one of his most important investors, standing in the doorway.

"I surrender." David scooped the paper up from the floor and tossed it back at Nathaniel. David was, as always, impeccably dressed in a blue coat he probably considered plain, though it was toggled and braided, and his waistcoat was covered in embroidery.

Nathaniel caught the ball of paper easily and tried to smooth it out. "Did you hear?" He motioned to the paper. "Morley had that fool son of his deliver a letter personally." Winthrop Morley was insufferable. David's father was a marquess—far above a provincial governor—and *he'd* never asked Nathaniel to bow and scrape. Winthrop was content to throw his father's name around and let better men do all the hard work.

David shook his head in disgust. "I heard rumors in the coffee room this morning. Governor Morley can't possibly stop all contraband tea from coming into Philadelphia."

"He intends to," Nathaniel growled. "This newfound loyalty he's mustered to king and country is surprising. He's been turning a blind eye to smuggling for the last decade."

"I heard the custom houses promised Morley a cut of all the East India Company tea sold at market. By keeping smuggled tea out, he ensures high demand for the legal variety."

Nathaniel slapped his desk. "I knew there was something in it for him!"

David pulled the chair in front of Nathaniel's desk back as much as possible and folded himself into the small space. To Nathaniel, who'd lived aboard ships most of his life, the snug office at the back of his warehouse was nearly palatial, possessing a desk, two chairs, a large framed map of the known world, and a lantern for working late nights.

David wrinkled his nose in distaste as he examined the unornamented wooden arms of his seat. "When that load of Madeira sells, you must purchase yourself better chairs with the profits."

Nathaniel had never been softened by the luxuries David insisted on. "The *Raleigh* departed only a month ago. We'll not see her return before next year, and by that time, I may need the profit to recover my losses from this tea catastrophe." His third ship, the *Fair Albion,* was undergoing repairs. He leaned back in his chair, which truthfully wasn't very comfortable.

"What do you mean to do?"

Nathaniel rubbed his forehead. "I must bring the tea to market despite the governor's interference."

"You must not involve yourself in anything unlawful," David admonished. "Smugglers are subject to a hefty fine, not to mention the loss of all the smuggled goods."

Nathaniel gave David a stern look. "Nine out of every ten cases of tea in this city have been brought in unlawfully. You've had no problem with my smuggling before now."

David shrugged. "That was before the governor decided he cared! Smuggling didn't really seem like a crime before. You'll have to find something else to do with it."

"There is nothing else. The Southern colonies will not purchase what they deem 'inferior' Dutch tea. Boston and New York already have established supply lines, and their markets cannot easily bear more."

"Store it in New Jersey?"

"Too expensive, and everyone will think of that. When all the merchants in this town grow desperate enough in a month or two, each will try to smuggle it in at once, and the market will flood with tea. If we want to turn a profit or avoid a total loss, we must act quickly."

"You could just pay the taxes." Spoken like a man who never had to think about money.

"We'd record a loss." How had he gotten started nattering on in such a way? He knew better than to worry an investor with pessimistic talk. He smiled tightly. "I'm sure it will all resolve."

David got to his feet. "Well, I've trusted you thus far, and you have amply repaid me. Are you changing before dinner?"

Nathaniel had forgotten all about David's birthday dinner. "Actually, I think it would be best if I stayed here and worked on a plan to bring the tea in without interference."

"I don't suppose every merchant in Philadelphia will

determine how to overtake you if you allow yourself one afternoon to celebrate the birthday of your greatest investor!"

Nathaniel wasn't sure what to say. He didn't want to offend such an important financial backer, but he didn't relish spending an afternoon in awkward and forced conversation with David's sister-in-law. David's wife was pleasant enough, but Helen was a termagant.

The first time Nathaniel had seen her, he'd been so struck by her loveliness he'd hardly known what to say. Though he'd regained his confidence in her presence since then, he'd taken to trying to speak to her as little as possible so as not to draw her ire.

He couldn't fathom why Helen disliked him so much when he'd been nothing but courteous to her each time they met. He'd even saved her life once by thumping her on the back when she was choking on a piece of cake.

Knowing he probably wasn't escaping the dinner, Nathaniel still made one final attempt. "I'm sure you could celebrate adequately without me."

"You're integral to the proceedings," David insisted. "Besides, a single man like yourself should jump at the chance to dine with a beautiful young lady."

Why would David say such a thing when Helen's dislike was quite apparent? "It sounds as if you're trying to foist your sister-in-law off on me."

David appeared to consider the idea seriously. "It would save me a great deal in housing and feeding her, not to mention her clothing. Excellent idea."

Nathaniel shifted in his seat. Helen was very pretty, and any other man might dream of having such a bride—but marriage wasn't in his plans, even if the lady in question didn't loathe him. "I've no need of a wife. My time is spent on my work."

"What if a wife could make your life more comfortable?"

David made it sound as if comfort was the most critical consideration in life. "I eat my dinner at the tavern; I pay a woman to launder my clothing. I mend my own tack, and I don't entertain guests. A wife would be far more costly than what I would get in return."

"That's one way to see things," David said solemnly, though there was laughter in his eyes. "No need to worry; I'm not ready to throw my sister-in-law away on just anyone. I have a whole series of tests planned for any likely candidates." David rubbed his hands together, evidently relishing the prospect.

There was another reason Nathaniel wouldn't think of courting Helen, even if he suffered a sudden change of heart about matrimony. Though David inexplicably desired his company at dinner, Nathaniel wasn't of the same social standing. What could he possibly have to recommend himself to Helen? She'd likely wish to marry someone who could provide the same luxuries she enjoyed in David's home.

David sat watching him expectantly, so Nathaniel slid into his plain black coat. "I gather you won't change your clothing. Very well, follow me to my home."

They stepped out of the warehouse, David waiting so Nathaniel could lock the door behind him. He would have to find another place to store the contraband tea, as this location was the first place the governor would search.

Door secured, the two men set out. Nathaniel liked the red-bricked city—especially the smooth, cobbled roads. They made carrying cargo from the docks to the warehouse much easier.

David wrinkled his nose distastefully. "I'll never grow accustomed to this odor."

Dock Creek was useful for moving goods from the Delaware River even further into the city, but the city's refuse had given the creek a pungent smell. "They didn't have odors in England, of course," Nathaniel retorted.

Though Nathaniel's tone was dry, David readily caught his sarcasm. "I am certain they must have, but I was never forced to endure them!" he returned. His ability to laugh at himself made David far more personable than any other wealthy man Nathaniel knew.

After a brisk walk west through the center of town, the men entered a brick row building and bypassed the lawyer's office on the ground floor.

David let Nathaniel into his apartment at the top of the stairs, then motioned for the drawing room. "Wait in there while I go find my wife."

Nathaniel dutifully entered the room and nearly turned around to walk out again. Helen Crofton was standing at the fireplace, back turned to him. Could he hide in the antechamber until David returned? He hated to set her bristles up before the dinner even started.

Helen turned and caught sight of him. "Oh!" She curtsied. "Welcome to our home. Do you wish to sit?"

Nathaniel bowed as courtesy demanded and settled in a corner chair he'd not seen on previous visits.

Helen settled onto the couch and arranged her skirt. Had the pink silk of her gown been made in Pennsylvania? It was very becoming. Perhaps there was something to American silk after all.

She smiled politely. "It's kind of you to come and celebrate David's birthday with us."

She needn't credit him for altruistic motives when David had practically dragged him out of the office. Nathaniel shrugged. "He insisted." Helen's eyes widened slightly, then she focused her attention on her folded hands.

After that, they sat in silence for some minutes, long enough that it became amusing to Nathaniel to imagine who would speak next.

Helen's eyes flicked to his face. "Do you care to explain your smile, Captain?"

Nathaniel stiffened at her words. "I'm not currently the captain of a vessel."

Her gaze became curious. "I thought once a captain, always a captain."

He shook his head but didn't elaborate, unsure how to explain that being the captain of a vessel was a pleasure he keenly missed. He'd not assume the title when he was forced to stay on land.

Helen glanced at the mantel clock. Did she expect him to raise another topic of conversation? He wasn't sure what courtesy demanded.

Before he could decide, Cassandra Beaufort swept into the room. "Captain Carter! Thank you for coming to celebrate my husband's birthday."

"The pleasure is all mine, I assure you." He bowed over her hand, grateful for Mrs. Beaufort's rescue from such an uncomfortable conversation. She wore a blue silk a few shades lighter than the color of the living room walls. He supposed David favored the color.

David stepped into the room after her. He'd changed into a white coat embroidered with a gold scroll pattern and a very expensive-looking wig. Perhaps Nathaniel should have gone home for his other, more formal black coat with the silver buttons. "Ah! Do you like my new chair? It's a Chippendale."

Nathaniel hadn't noticed anything extraordinary about it. "Very nice."

David waved a hand at his wife. "And Cassandra's gown—Pennsylvania silk. Let's hear your arguments against the venture now!"

"Helen's gown also," Cassandra prompted her husband.

"How silly of me—isn't Helen lovely?" David looked expectantly at Nathaniel.

Nathaniel couldn't argue with that, nor was he too proud to own he'd been wrong. He grinned in self-mockery. "The silk is far better than I imagined."

"Well." David's laugh seemed a little forced, and Nathaniel realized too late he should've confirmed David's compliment to the ladies.

Before Nathaniel could say anything to rectify his mistake, David motioned them through to the drawing room. "I believe dinner is laid out if you care to follow me?"

Nathaniel glanced at Helen, unsure if he should offer his arm. She stepped past him without glancing his way, making it clear how much she wanted his assistance. Unsurprising that an accomplished lady would wish nothing to do with an uncouth sea captain, too ill-mannered to make polite conversation.

Although he'd tried to get out of attending, Nathaniel found he could do great service to the meal laid before him. The family kept an excellent cook, and Westing, David's valet, hovered in the corner, watching for any chance to be of service to the family.

Cassandra attempted to make conversation with Nathaniel

by inquiring about his business. "Do you have any voyages planned?"

"Now that I own three ships, I must coordinate the business of all, and I can't do that separated from the post for months at a time."

Helen surprised him by voicing a question about his work. "Do you miss it? Being a captain, I mean."

Nathaniel smiled wistfully. "I miss the order of my ship and always knowing exactly what I must do next." There were only so many things that could go wrong on a ship and a finite number of things to do in response, but it would be difficult to explain how relaxing he found that.

His dinner companions made sympathetic faces, and he hurried to change the subject. He hadn't intended to cast a pall over the meal. "I don't miss the hardtack. This is far more to my taste." He held up a fresh roll to prove his point. Westing seemed to take that as a sign he wanted more bread and rushed forward with a basket.

David turned to Helen. "How was the Young Society Ladies Meeting?"

"Philadelphia Young Ladies Charitable Society," she corrected. "The meeting was very productive."

Cassandra swatted playfully at her sister. "She neglects to add that she was elected president."

David clapped. "Good for you!"

Helen's lips twisted in an effort to fight off a proud smile. "And we agreed on a new project to buy out the indenture of a young lady who is in a very desperate circumstance."

"We mean to sell gooseberry tarts at High Street Market," Cassandra added.

David nodded in approval. "Excellent choice. Gooseberries are very fashionable."

"Just what I said!" Helen beamed at David. "I want so much to do a good job as president, and I can hardly think of a better cause to take up."

Nathaniel watched Helen's eager expression and wondered if she'd accept a little advice. He might not have much to offer by way of compliments, but business knowledge was another matter. "An indenture is quite dear," he ventured. He started to do some calculations in his mind. "You must mean to sell a great number of pies, and the market is only open two days a week."

Helen's smile slipped a little. "Tarts, you mean. I've not precisely calculated how many we must sell, but I'm certain we can manage to raise the funds we need. The market is always crowded."

No matter the demand, she needed to price the tarts correctly to turn a profit. Then there were the expenses to think of. "High Street Market stalls are very dear. Have you considered New Market?"

"High Street has more traffic," Helen returned.

Nathaniel continued to mull over her problem. He didn't transport much produce and never anything that could be obtained locally, but he didn't imagine gooseberries were in season during the autumn. "Where will you get the fruit?"

"We'll use preserves." She placed her fork down. "I thank you for your help, but I'm certain we're capable of managing everything without assistance."

"You'll need to learn from someone if you want your business to succeed," David interjected. "Or perhaps you should ask for donations."

Nathaniel frowned. He hadn't much to spare at the moment. "I will pledge five pence to you," he offered.

Helen lost any pretense of a smile. "I don't intend to take a ha'penny from you or any other man. We will do this ourselves."

Nathaniel blinked in astonishment. He'd only been trying to help. Why was she so averse to a bit of advice from someone far more experienced in business matters?

David looked from Nathaniel to Helen and then cleared his throat. "I attended a meeting today of a private organization that wants to free the colonies from unfair taxation."

"We all know you speak of the Sons of Liberty," Helen scoffed.

David narrowed his eyes at her. "This *private* organization means to host an assembly to determine what to do about the Tea Act which Parliament saw fit to pass."

Nathaniel forced his attention away from Helen and to his host. "I know of the Sons of Liberty, and I would not trust a one of them to keep his word, not after what happened in Boston a few years ago."

"That was unfortunate," David admitted. "Though most of the merchants did stick to the agreement not to import the English goods."

"You were still in England then." Nathaniel took a sip of wine. "I won't be making any decisions based on the paper promises of that lot."

David inclined his head in acknowledgment. "I think most of them are very sincere, and only a handful of merchants went back on their word. Most of the Sons of Liberty believe in promoting freedom."

"Aye—freedom for themselves, to make as much money as they can," Nathaniel replied. "Though perhaps that's the noblest cause of all."

Helen watched the debate closely. "You don't seem to believe anyone can accomplish anything. You must have had a very sad upbringing."

Cassandra blanched. "Helen!"

"I had a perfectly normal boyhood." No need to mention his father had died when Nathaniel was only seven or that his mother had given him to his uncle to employ on a ship shortly after so she could marry a local widower. He'd known people who'd risen from even starker conditions, though perhaps a lady who'd never known more hardship than a lost stocking would think his childhood tragic.

Helen looked at her plate. "My apologies for my rudeness."

Nathaniel only nodded in acknowledgment. He couldn't claim to be surprised by her treatment. She'd made her distaste for him clear from their very first meeting.

After dinner, he declined to stay for champagne or coffee. "I've plans to develop," he said by way of an excuse.

David walked him out to the street. "I thank you for coming. Will you shake hands with me, or have I done you too great a mischief by forcing you to endure Helen's company?"

"I will shake, and gladly. No harm was done to me."

"I don't know why you bring out the worst in Helen. She's really a pleasant companion most of the time."

Nathaniel snorted in amusement. "All the better she remains in your household."

He bowed to his host and made his way down the street. Helen Crofton's opinions didn't matter to him in the least. He didn't have time to pay her any more mind.

He turned his thoughts towards what he would have to do to get his tea into the city.

Chapter 3

The first market day after the society meeting, Helen set off with her cousin Constance to find the perfect location to sell tarts. Helen had asked Cassandra, but her sister had promised to spend the morning returning calls with David. While Constance might not have been much practical use, Helen liked her dreamy cousin, and she didn't need more than her company. She'd already detailed the tart plan so thoroughly not even Captain Carter could find fault with it.

Even after two days, Helen hadn't managed to forget the awkward dinner or that Captain Carter hadn't been able to muster a word of encouragement—not for her appearance when David had nearly begged him to compliment her, and not for the Society's tart scheme. He'd only lobbed pessimistic observations. She couldn't know if his disdain was personally directed at her or if he assumed all ladies were useless, but he'd made his doubt in her success perfectly clear.

Constance rubbed her arms under her cloak. "It's hardly warmer in the market than on the street."

Helen pulled her cloak tighter around herself. The enormous High Street Market consisted of stalls under a series of covered sheds, but the roof overhead did nothing to cut the chill on a windy October day. "Let's hurry and find something so we can go home." She looked down the line of vendors until she spotted a baker with bread and rolls but no tarts.

She tried her finely crafted smile on the baker. "Would you rent me space in your stall?"

The baker, a stout man with a square jaw, scrutinized her in return. "What are you selling?"

"Tarts." He raised an eyebrow. "Gooseberry tarts," Helen quickly amended. "For charitable purposes." Hopefully, mentioning the noble cause would soften his heart.

"Five shillings each market day, and you can use that." The baker shoved a finger to a rough wooden table that stuck out into the thoroughfare.

Five shillings? They'd have to sell nearly thirty slices just to make the rent! "Thank you, but that's more money than we have to spend. Come, Constance."

The market was crowded with servants fulfilling commissions for their employers and fashionable ladies shopping for trinkets. Fearing she'd lose her absentminded cousin, Helen held Constance's elbow as they wove through the main thoroughfare in pursuit of suitable places to sell tarts.

After nearly two hours of searching, five shillings turned out to be quite the best rate, even after they expanded their search to more than just bakers. One woman quoted them two pounds for a corner on the edge of her vegetable cart! Most of the vendors weren't remotely interested in losing any space for their own wares.

Helen bit her lip. Perhaps she should go back and accept

the first man's terms, or perhaps the high price should be discussed by the society before she could enter into an agreement.

Helen's companion seemed to have withdrawn into a more congenial inner world. "Do you not think it would be the loveliest thing in the world for two people to meet at a bakery stall and fall in love?" Constance was always half-in, half-out of a daydream on account of Aunt Anne allowing her daughters to read sentimental novels. Helen's governess had never permitted such vain pursuits.

Helen, busy trying to work out what to do, tried not to show her impatience. "I'm afraid I fail to see the appeal in that."

"It's appealing because it would be so unexpected. A young lady—perhaps an indentured servant—goes to buy the family bread. While there, she chances to meet a sea captain, on leave for a few days only. They look into each other's eyes, and the captain falls instantly in love with her! He pays off her indenture, and they marry at once!" Constance clasped her hands above her heart.

Helen managed to turn a disbelieving laugh into a cough. "And then he goes off for months at a time, forgets to send her any money, and she's worse off than she was before, for now, she has a landlord dunning her and nothing to eat."

Constance stared at Helen in astonishment, seemingly at a loss for words.

"It doesn't fit with my experience of life. Nothing ever works out so neatly."

"It did for your sister," Constance argued.

Helen didn't bother to hide her laugh. "David was odious to Cassandra and me when we first met. He didn't want anything to do with us. It was only after he saw how perfect she is that he melted."

"That was still very unlikely then, wasn't it? And that proves that two people could fall in love in front of a bread stall."

"Perhaps." Helen adjusted her gray wool cloak and continued walking, looking for any stalls they might have missed.

"It would be just the thing for a romance!"

Helen thought she recognized the man standing at the end of the row. Captain Carter's broad shoulders encased in his customary stark black coat stood out even in the crowded market. "Oh, no!"

Constance flinched as if she'd been struck. "I say it would!"

"No, not your story. Quick, walk this way." Helen didn't need his cynical observations to add to an already disappointing morning. She steered Constance around him, striding purposefully as if she had a very important destination ahead.

"Good day."

Helen sighed and turned around. "Captain Carter." She supposed her fetching cap ribbons had drawn his attention. She shouldn't have fed her vanity by keeping her hood down.

"Oh!" Constance looked up at him like he was a character who had stepped right off the page of a romance. As if a chiseled face and statuesque physique were all that mattered in a man.

Constance elbowed Helen hard in the stomach and cast her eyes repeatedly towards Captain Carter.

Helen begrudgingly obliged her cousin. "This is Captain Carter. Captain Carter, this is Miss Constance Hayes." Constance beamed at him and curtsied deeply, while Helen's curtsy could have been mistaken for a slight spasm in her leg.

A man as rude in spirit as Captain Carter had no business

looking so appealing cutting a bow. "Pleased to make your acquaintance. Do I guess correctly—you are doing the work of the Young Ladies of Philadelphia?"

Had he intentionally mixed up the name to make it sound like a social club rather than a serious philanthropic organization? Helen prayed silently for patience. "Philadelphia Young Ladies Charitable Society," she corrected, voice tight.

"Yes, we have been walking to and fro quite as much as the adversary himself trying to find a place to sell our gooseberry tarts." Constance seemed much more attuned to the conversation than she had been all morning.

Captain Carter smiled broadly at the joke, and Helen wrinkled her nose in surprise. The comment hadn't been funny enough to merit the merriest smile she'd yet observed on the captain's face during the three years of their acquaintance.

"What would you advise us to do? I'm sure a sea captain must know ever so much about buying and selling." Constance's eyes were veritably sparkling with admiration. Was her cousin fixing Captain Carter in her mind as the hero of the romance she was dreaming about?

That was not to be borne. "We really must continue on. Good day." Helen started to walk forward, but Constance didn't follow.

"The owners who sell in this part of the market hold their spaces very dear. How much have you to spend?" Captain Carter sounded as if he were genuinely concerned, but Helen guessed he was searching for another opportunity to offer the benefit of his advice.

"We only have ten shillings from all our dues," Constance confided. "We were hoping to pay a sixpence each day."

Constance seemed perfectly willing to give away all of the business of the society to a perfect stranger. Would that Captain Carter would have the grace to mind his own business and that her cousin would mind her tongue! Helen caught herself tapping her foot in impatience and forced herself to be still. Mama had always said a lady ought to be serene no matter the circumstance.

Captain Carter frowned, an expression Helen had seen far more often—usually directed at her. "The only place that would give you space at that rate would be in the fish market, but of course, you wouldn't want that."

The fish market! Why hadn't she thought of it? The smelly fish vendors would probably jump at the chance to rent space to them at a low rate. "That's precisely where we're headed, incidentally," Helen lied.

He laughed outright as if she'd made an excellent joke. "Nobody is going to buy slices of gooseberry pie surrounded by the stench of fish, even if you could convince the Charitable Ladies to stomach it long enough to hawk their wares."

Helen didn't appreciate being made sport of. "Everyone likes tarts—even people buying fish. They might actually hold it all the more dear for not having to walk to the main market." Captain Carter raised an eyebrow. Did he think the only opinions that mattered were his own? "Once our reputation for selling the best-tasting pastries in Philadelphia grows, we'll have customers lined up for miles, fish or no fish!"

He stared at her incredulously. "Ah, well, you are certainly the expert. A lowly businessman such as I could not dream of teaching you anything about business you do not already know." He swept another bow and started off in the other direction, shoulders stiff.

Constance stared after him. "I think you've offended him."

What did he have to be offended about? "Come. It's rude to stare at a gentleman." Helen glanced back at Captain Carter. "Well, a man, anyway. I'm not certain you could call Captain Carter a gentleman." She regretted the insult as soon as the words were out of her mouth. She was being churlish, just as she'd been when she accused him of having a difficult upbringing. "Forget I said that."

Constance didn't seem to have noticed either the insult or the apology. "A sea captain," she murmured to herself. No question about it, Constance had found a new subject for her imaginings.

The cousins walked two blocks to the fish market, where the odor was overpowering long before they could see the stalls.

Constance was already looking green. "Are you certain about this?" Helen asked. "I could come back without you." Or perhaps give up the whole scheme. If Constance couldn't even manage to inquire about a stall, that didn't bode well for the society being able to sell tarts.

"I'm fine," Constance croaked. She pulled her kerchief over her nose.

Helen eyed Constance uncertainly. "If you're sure . . ." Helen led her cousin forward through the rows of stalls selling fish, turtles, and other sea creatures. Blood soaked the tables while flies buzzed around entrails in swarms. They couldn't sell tarts amidst such filth!

Helen nearly despaired of finding a suitable spot as they walked down the long rows. Only the thought of how smug Captain Carter would be if he discovered she'd quit gave her the strength to press on.

Finally, she spotted a small, empty hut at the end of a row. "Excuse me?" she called into the next stall over.

"Aye?"

"Do you know who owns this?" Helen pointed to the empty hut.

"Aye."

A long silence ensued. "Might you tell me who?"

"'Tis mine."

"Would you rent it to me?" Helen managed to croak.

The man stared at her as if he didn't understand what she was saying. Helen was horrified to realize he had fish bones and gore in his long beard. She took one step backward. They should never have come.

The man chose that moment to reply. "Sixpence a day. Roof leaks when it rains."

"Oh, that is an excellent price! I mean, it seems very fair." They would still have funds left over for ingredients.

The sound of retching made her turn around. Constance was losing her last meal onto the pavement. Helen thought she was in danger of doing so herself, so overpowering was the fishy odor.

"We'll start on Monday. I'll bring the money with me. Good day!"

Helen managed to get Constance home. To her relief, the Hayes family didn't seem terribly surprised to see her cousin's pale face, saying she'd always possessed a weak stomach. Perhaps the other ladies would manage to overcome the fish scent after getting used to it. After apologizing profusely, Helen retreated to her own home.

The day hadn't ended auspiciously, but setbacks were to be expected. As long as she persisted—and if she could keep certain interfering persons from preventing her—all would be well. She turned her attention to studying her mother's receipt book. Compared to finding a stall, baking tarts would be easy.

Chapter 4

Nathaniel tried to shake off his irritating encounter with Helen so he could get back to work. He'd been civil to her and offered sound advice, yet she'd responded by scorning him—again. He couldn't remember anyone, not even his fiercest competitors, treating him in such a manner. Even her dreamy cousin had attended more closely to his words than Helen had.

He'd grown a successful business from nothing, and still, his assistance was worth less than the dirt beneath her feet. It couldn't only be the difference in their statuses that influenced her to scorn him—David didn't seem to have any problem with him.

As he walked away from the market, Winthrop Morley appeared. He wore a vivid orange silk coat that stuck out as much for its color as for how ostentatious it was for a market. "Carter. How nice to see you." A blatant lie, but Nathaniel didn't wish to prolong the conversation by pointing out the untruth.

"Morley." Nathaniel bowed and made to go on.

"How intriguing to find you here rather than in that quaint little warehouse I had the privilege of visiting the other day." Winthrop scrutinized him as if looking for the answer to a complex puzzle.

Nathaniel had paid for that "quaint little warehouse" with his own blood and sweat, which was more than Winthrop could likely say about anything he owned, but he once more ignored as much of Winthrop's words as he could. "This is a public market. I've a right to be here as much as you do."

"Do you know what I think?" Winthrop placed a hand on his hip. "I think you're scouting locations where you can sell your contraband wares. What do you say to that?"

"I say you should take care not to exhaust your reasoning ability when it's obviously in limited supply. Good day." He walked on without looking back, though he could imagine Winthrop's expression showed a mix of horror and anger at having been insulted.

In truth, Winthrop wasn't far wrong, though Nathaniel already knew what merchants he could count on to take possession of the tea. The trouble was delivering the product without getting caught. Unloading the cases from barges on the river into whatever location he managed to secure would be difficult enough with the constabulary roaming about under the governor's orders. Nathaniel couldn't count on more than one hour on one dark night to get the tea into Philadelphia.

To evade discovery in the final stage of his plan, Nathaniel would bring disguised barrels of tea to the market as if he was just another vendor coming to town on a market day, then deliver them to his buyers. If he managed to pull it off, his maneuverings would render the tea's origin inscrutable. That morning he'd observed the timing of deliveries to and from the market, but he needed to visit a few more times before deciding to execute his plan in the morning when many deliveries and larger crowds lent anonymity, or later in the day when there were fewer people to observe. Apparently, he also had Winthrop to contend with, but avoiding the miscreant shouldn't prove much difficulty.

Before all else, Nathaniel had to secure a way for the tea to travel up the Delaware River to Philadelphia. Previously, he'd hired day laborers to bring in his cargo, all legal and aboveboard. Now that the governor was putting his foot down, he had to turn to a different sort of worker.

The sign over the door of the Devil's Punchbowl was so dirty Nathaniel walked past the tavern a few times before finally recognizing it as his destination. The entrance to the place required a step down into an establishment reminiscent of a dungeon. With no windows and smoke rolling out of the fireplace, it was nearly impossible to make out who anyone was.

Nathaniel pulled out a chair to await his contact, hoping the infernal character of the place wasn't an ill omen.

"Carter?" a voice rasped.

"Aye?"

"Matlack." The man who addressed Nathaniel didn't offer his hand before planting himself in the chair opposite. He was grizzled from too many days in the sun, with dirty white hair and several long scars across his face.

"I need delivery of forty chests from my ship in Chester to a warehouse in the city." Best to get to the point and leave the filthy tavern as quickly as possible.

The man's lips split into what was probably supposed to be a smile. "The kind of delivery that takes place at night when no one else is around, I presume?"

"Aye."

Matlack leaned forward. "And you're prepared to pay?"

"Upon delivery." Nathaniel had been in business long enough to know not to trust the man sitting before him with as much as a penny before the goods were safely stowed.

Matlack pulled out a large knife and started cleaning under his nails. "My men won't be too keen on putting their faith in you."

Nathaniel inclined his head. "Nevertheless, I won't pay until the tea is delivered."

"My men will want to know if you'll talk all over town and bring the governor on our heads."

"I've no desire to be caught smuggling."

Matlack pointed the tip of his knife at Nathaniel. "You'll ride along with us on the barges."

That suited Nathaniel fine: he'd be able to see that his tea didn't disappear. "Very well."

"And you'll have one of your men at the docks to signal all clear," Matlack added. "Two lanterns if it's safe and one if it's not. If it's not safe, we dump the cargo and speed back to Chester before the constable can round us up."

Nathaniel paused. He didn't have employees that worked for him consistently besides his captains, who hired their own crews. Captain Eaker was halfway to Cadiz, Captain Jones was visiting family in Charleston, and Captain Henrickson moved too slowly on a stiff leg to run from the constabulary if it came to that.

"Problem?" Matlack leered at him, and Nathaniel suppressed a shiver.

"No problem." He would find someone.

Matlack spat into his hand and extended it to Nathaniel, who omitted his own secretion but shook nonetheless.

He wandered out into the street and pondered who he could ask to wait at the dock. He didn't have employees to ask, and he had no real friends. At the end of the day, there was only one person in the world he trusted implicitly—himself.

Perhaps David was right, and he should just forget about the tea. Every day the ship sat in the harbor at Chester was another day of losing money. He could dump all the cases and send the *Good King George* to Europe for a legal product.

The potential profit was enormous if he could avoid getting caught. The newly taxed legal tea imports hadn't even arrived yet, so shopkeepers were already running low and were willing to pay more than usual. If he could only pull this off one time, he wouldn't have to attempt it again.

Nathaniel shook his head in disgust with himself. He hadn't gained the ownership of three ships by fretting over them. After securing his first position, his uncle had not interceded in his life again. Nathaniel had learned to rely on himself, stay alert to the way others achieved success, and copy them. He'd managed to work his way up from cabin boy to captain to owner by the age of twenty-nine. If he could do all that, he could manage to find one man to hold a lantern or two at the dock.

Chapter 5

The day after her quasi-successful trip to the market, Helen invaded the apartment kitchen. She'd been on the lookout for Peggy, the cook, to visit a friend so she could practice her tart making in private. Peggy hadn't left until dinner was removed, which didn't leave Helen much time to attempt the tart before attending a concert at Euphemia's later that evening.

Helen poured over her mother's receipt for fruit tarts and wondered what constituted a "goodly" quantity of goose fat. She picked through the kitchen shelves until she found a jar filled with pale yellow fat that smelled of animal, then took a long wooden spoon and scooped a large amount into her mixing bowl. After the goose fat came several heaping spoonfuls of flour, which Helen hoped sufficed a "generous measure." To her dismay, it was challenging to combine the flour and fat with the wooden spoon, and when the concoction didn't roll out the way it ought, she was forced to press the crust into a shallow pan with her fingers.

After digging a few minutes among Peggy's carefully ordered

ingredients, Helen managed to locate gooseberry jam at the back of a shelf and spooned it over the crust. The entire jar of jam only made a thin, pitiful layer on top of the tart. Perhaps the whole thing would puff up while it baked?

She carried the pan to the oven, only to discover that instead of being perfectly heated from Peggy's earlier baking, the beehive oven was barely warm and already full of meat pies. Helen frowned to herself. The receipt book said to build a healthy blaze, but the logs beneath the oven were merely glowing. Perhaps Peggy hadn't realized her fire would die down quite as much.

Helen wedged her tart into the last space in the oven and built up the fire. Once she was sure it wouldn't go out, she turned her attention to the worktable, covered in flour and sticky dough from her failed attempt to roll out the crust. Peggy would be furious to come home to such a mess. Helen scraped and wiped the table over and over until it was finally clean, then went to refill the water pail from the pump in the square.

She wiped her forehead with her apron, over warm from bustling about the kitchen despite the coolness of the day, then went to see about her tart. Her stomach dropped the moment she opened the oven door. The tart resembled a three-day-old stew—globs of gooseberry jam swam in puddles of greasy liquid, and various portions of the crust had bubbled up like dumplings. Helen groaned. She'd never be able to hold her head up at the society if she couldn't manage a single tart.

She turned back to her mother's book for an indication of what to do next. The receipt said to bake until the center of the tart bubbled. Helen scrutinized the tart, but she couldn't detect any such activity. Hoping all the tart needed was a little more baking, she went to prepare a gown for Euphemia's concert.

Helen fanned her face while she perused the garments in her clothes press. Would it be more appropriate to wear a green velvet robe or the pink silk she'd worn to David's birthday dinner? She was about to ask Cassandra's opinion when the sound of raised voices startled her back into the kitchen.

"What in the name of the Almighty has happened?" Peggy screamed. Black smoke rolled off from the closed oven in waves.

Helen ran forward to throw open the oven door just as Westing leaped into the room and began fanning furiously at the smoke with a cloth. "I'm sorry, Peggy; I was only trying to bake a tart."

"Get out of me way!" Peggy pushed Helen aside and grabbed at the tart with her bare hands. She threw it down on the worktable and then started pulling out the meat pies. "A week's worth of baking up in flames." The last of the pies she withdrew actually was on fire.

Peggy's lips pressed tightly together as she glared at Helen and fanned the smoke. Even gentle Westing offered Helen a mildly censorious look.

Helen was too ashamed to speak. She could only gape at her ruined dessert, charred black as if it had been made of coals.

David appeared at the door, waving smoke and coughing. "What's going on here?"

"My tart—" Helen whispered.

David didn't wait for more of an answer. "We must open all the windows." He and Westing disappeared into the corridor, and Helen ran to open the door to the apartment. Below, standing at the entrance of his law office, stood Uncle Josiah.

"Is anything the matter?" he inquired.

"Just a burnt tart," Helen explained, coughing in her sleeve. "We have everything under control." Another gentleman stepped out from behind Uncle Josiah. Governor Morley—How mortifying!

"My apologies." Helen stepped back into the apartment and hoped he didn't recognize her.

The sound of a low moan had her running down the corridor. She burst into Cassandra's room without waiting to knock. Her sister was kneeling over a chamber pot, moaning and retching.

"You've made her very ill," David snapped. He had a hand on Cassandra's back.

"I'm sorry—may I—" Helen took two steps into the room.

David scowled at her. "Just leave us alone!"

Helen spun and ran from the room. Her bedroom was tiny compared to the one she'd occupied on her father's estate in England, though she knew it had once been shared by several of the Hayes girls years ago when the family lived above Uncle Josiah's law office.

She threw herself on her bed, stared at the ceiling, and tried to determine what she should do next. Should she admit defeat and tell the ladies of the society they'd have to cancel the whole scheme just because she couldn't manage to bank a single tart?

Captain Carter would be delighted to be proven correct about her.

Helen sat up. Captain Carter was wrong. He might know something about teas and silks, but he was not an expert on tarts.

Euphemia was also supposed to practice baking. Perhaps

she had succeeded. Helen would go to her concert and sample a lovely tart, and all would be well.

It had to be. She couldn't let that poor indentured servant down, nor face telling everyone how inept she was.

Chapter 6

Nathaniel sighed heavily as he knocked on the Goodwins' front door. Though he wasn't looking forward to the evening's entertainments, he'd changed into the coat he saved for important occasions—black, like his everyday coat, but with embossed silver buttons. Nothing like what David wore, of course, but Nathaniel wasn't trying to impress anyone, just appease Goodwin, another of his investors.

A servant admitted him into the home and led him to the library, where Humphrey Goodwin and the other male guests were drinking spirits before the musical portion of the evening.

"Ah, Carter." Goodwin thumped Nathaniel's back. "I despaired of seeing you tonight, but you're much too shrewd a businessman to risk offending me! Not that I blame you for wanting to stay away. From what I've heard of her lessons, Euphemia has improved since last year's concert, but sitting through all that nonsense is always a dead bore."

Nathaniel wasn't sure how to respond, as affirming his

host's words seemed ungentlemanly, so he settled on a nod.

"Nathaniel." David joined their party by the door of the library.

Goodwin addressed David in a low voice. "How are you suffering under this shocking turn of events?"

David raised an eyebrow. "Suffering?"

"The tea issue, what else?" Goodwin stared incredulously at David as if shocked the younger man wasn't similarly fixated on the matter. "I stand to lose a great deal of money if Carter doesn't pull off his little scheme."

Nathaniel shuffled his feet. Goodwin had demanded his entire investment back in cash when he'd heard of the Governor's order, forcing Nathaniel to bring the man in on his plan to recoup their outlay.

"Oh." David waved a hand. "I have the utmost confidence in Mr. Carter." Nathaniel smiled gratefully at David, despite a churning in his stomach. If he failed, he'd lose both David's confidence and his money.

Goodwin raised a skeptical eyebrow at Nathaniel. "How is the plan coming along?"

"I've found a team of men who are used to working silently in the dark."

"Oh-ho, that will show old Morley!" Goodwin exclaimed.

David stiffened and tipped his head. "Remember, the man's son is sitting just there."

Nathaniel glanced across the room and saw Winthrop Morley stared right at them.

"Let him hear," Goodwin chortled. "Morley's not a bad fellow, but he's overstepped this time. The colonies need more leeway than Parliament allows for. If Morley can't keep the peace, he'll be replaced."

David made a face. "I don't relish the business of smuggling. I fear it will end in disaster."

"Smuggling is so common in the colonies that it's practically patriotic," Nathaniel retorted.

David spread the hand not holding his drink. "It's grown more dangerous of late. What if there's another way?"

Goodwin broke in. "Say you don't mean relying on the Sons of Liberty! Their planned demonstration will come to naught just as it always has. Besides, I don't mind depriving the king of a few pounds, but I draw the line at rebellion. These colonies are English land for English people and English rule." He stuck his finger in the air at each utterance of his mother country's name.

Nathaniel couldn't risk offending the man by saying what he thought of King George. While he had no trust in the Sons of Liberty, he also felt no allegiance to a king he'd never seen.

"I daresay you look terribly suspicious there," a voice drawled. Nathaniel stiffened. Winthrop Morley had snuck up behind them.

"We are merely talking of the weather," David lied.

Winthrop smirked. "Of course; there's much to say. How cool it has been, and how characteristic of October." He turned to Nathaniel. "I thought to drop you a little hint. My father hoped that merely confiscating the ill-gotten goods of would-be smugglers would suffice, but he's heard rumors that not everyone finds that sufficient motivation. Tomorrow he'll make an announcement." He paused for dramatic effect. "Anyone caught smuggling will have *all* his assets seized on behalf of the crown."

Nathaniel and David exchanged a glance. Previously, the cost of smuggling was a fine and the loss of that ship's cargo.

Losing everything was a significantly harsher penalty.

Goodwin snorted. "Your father should take care not to strike a match that will send the whole tinderbox up in flame."

"My father is loyal to the king, and the king will reward that loyalty." Winthrop took a sip of his drink and then turned to Nathaniel. "I hope we'll run into each other at the market again. Perhaps you'd be so good as to let me shadow you? I've taken quite an interest in your operations, and I'm keen to discover exactly how you go on."

He nodded to Winthrop but remained silent. Winthrop's threat was apparent, but Nathaniel still needed to watch the market to determine exactly how to move the tea to his buyers. He'd have to be doubly careful not to allow Winthrop to know what he was up to.

A servant appeared at Goodwin's side. "Miss Euphemia says she means to come down soon, and she'd like all the gentlemen to be seated."

"I am loyal to my king, gentlemen," Goodwin said, "but I obey my daughter. Follow me!"

The men followed Goodwin to the drawing room, and Nathaniel selected a chair on the back row, mentally debating if he could leave during Miss Goodwin's first number or if politeness dictated he wait until intermission.

David took a seat next to his wife. They appeared to have left Helen at home. Not far from them, one of the Hayes daughters—Nathaniel didn't know them well enough to know which—appeared to be enacting a stage show maneuvering to sit next to Winthrop.

Euphemia swept into the room once everyone was seated. A hush fell over the assembled guests as she sat down at the harpsichord. She bowed her head as if in prayer and then threw her hands on the keys. She had admittedly improved since last year, but Nathaniel had to agree with Humphrey that such music was not to his taste.

A minute later, David made his way down the aisle supporting his wife. Nathaniel jumped up to see if he could be of assistance—and possibly take the opportunity to leave.

He closed the door behind the trio. "Everything all right?"

"Cassandra's not feeling very well, so we are leaving. May I trouble you to see Helen home? She's disappeared somewhere in this house."

"I can manage—" Cassandra said weakly before breaking down into a coughing fit.

"Your sister nearly murdered you! I think she's the one who must manage."

Nathaniel raised an eyebrow. Attempted murder? That must be an exaggeration. "Very well," he agreed reluctantly. He didn't want to spend any more time than he had to in Helen's company but felt he couldn't refuse. If he could find her, perhaps she would also want to leave early when she heard about her sister, and he could escape from the party by escorting her home.

David flashed a small smile. "I won't forget it." He ushered his wife outside.

Nathaniel made his way down the corridor of the main floor. He knew from previous visits that the dining room was behind a pair of ornate double doors, but it seemed unlikely Helen was in there.

He looked across the corridor to the room he'd vacated only a little earlier. Perhaps Helen was in the library? He turned the knob slowly, but before he could open the door, he heard a loud crash.

"Blast!" someone hissed. Nathaniel pushed the door open and found Helen kneeling in front of the fireplace, green velvet gown pooling around her. She was hurriedly picking up shards of what had been a vase from the mantel.

"Did you break that?"

Helen looked up in alarm at the sound of his voice, then looked back to her task when she recognized him. "I leaned against the mantel, and it fell down on my head."

Nathaniel closed the door behind himself before anyone else became aware of her mishap and walked forward to help.

"It would be you who discovered me," Helen muttered. "You can laugh at my downfall."

She certainly made no secret about how much she disliked him. "I hardly think breaking a vase constitutes a downfall." He glanced down at the shards he'd collected and noticed gold inlay that signified an expensive piece. He might've spoken too soon.

"It's not just that." Helen breathed a long sigh. "I might as well tell you myself. It's only fair to give you the satisfaction of being proved right. All the plans I had for the society are ruined. I couldn't manage to make a solitary gooseberry tart, and nor could Euphemia."

Nathaniel's brow wrinkled in confusion. "Why should that satisfy me?"

"Why should it not?" She shook her head at two fistfuls of shards, then looked around for a place to put them. "What am I to say to Euphemia?"

Nathaniel dropped his handfuls of shards into his coat pocket and reached for Helen's while thinking to himself that there was something to be said for a plain wool coat over a silk one, after all. "Probably best not to say anything."

Helen looked at him uncertainly. "I don't wish a servant to be blamed for my mistake."

Nathaniel tilted his head. It was a fair consideration. "You broke the vase while under my protection. I'll tell Goodwin there was an accident and offer to pay for it." Little though he wanted to give Goodwin another reason to be upset with him or owe the man any more money.

"Don't be ridiculous!" Helen scoffed. "What do you mean, under your protection?"

"Your sister had to leave early, and David asked me to escort you home." He beckoned again for her to hand over her collected shards.

"Very well, but there's no way I'm letting you pay for the vase." Helen dropped the shards into his outstretched hand. "I'll speak to Euphemia about it the next time I see her. Now, do you wish to stay longer at the party, or may we depart?"

There wasn't anything Nathaniel wanted more than to leave at once. "I'm at your disposal." Helen followed him out of the room. "Do you have a cloak to fetch?" he whispered. She shook her head, and they left the house without a word to anyone as Euphemia slammed out another piece.

"I don't have a coach," Nathaniel apologized. He couldn't imagine anyone in David's household was much used to walking long distances. "Can you manage the mile?"

"I walk to Pine Street at least once a week," Helen informed him, the heat in her voice alerting Nathaniel that he'd once again said the wrong thing. "I might not be able to make a tart, but I can put one foot in front of the other."

"Of course."

The street lights didn't allow him to make out the finer details of her face, but he saw when Helen looked sideways at him. "You're not as delighted as I imagined to hear me confirmed a hopeless failure."

Was he a regular subject in her imagination? "I don't recall ever naming you hopeless, nor a failure."

"But you do think it," she pressed. "You made that quite clear with all your criticisms of my plans for the society."

He'd never intended to cause offense. "I only meant to help! I ask myself difficult questions each and every time I begin a new venture. At least I have ever since my initial mistakes."

Helen made a noise of disbelief. "It's difficult to credit the notion you have great business failures lurking in your past."

He'd soon prove her wrong. "I lost money on the first cargo I ever brought in as an owner. I knew a great deal about ships and sailing, but nothing of business." He'd put everything he had into that first investment. Every penny he'd managed to scrape together, every favor he could leverage, and come away with almost nothing.

"Oh." Helen watched him with rapt attention he'd never before known from her. "How did you learn all you know?"

"By observation and asking questions, and from learning from my mistakes and not repeating them." He regretted his answer before he finished speaking. If Helen found his questions criticisms, she'd surely think such words meant to insult her.

To his astonishment, she laughed. "Very well, Captain—Mister—Carter. I take your lesson."

"I wasn't implying—"

She laid a hand on his arm and offered a soft smile. "Truly. I've taken no offense."

Nathaniel couldn't tear his eyes away from the sight of her smooth, pretty hand resting on his black coat until she removed it to slip her arm through his. She didn't seem to have any hesitation about taking his arm on the street.

He realized with a start that she'd spoken and was awaiting his response. "I'm sorry; what was that?"

Her amused laugh at his distraction sparked a thrill of delight through his body. "I said that I wished I'd discovered your true intent earlier when I could have salvaged the society's plans. There's no chance we'll succeed now." She said the last as if it was a piece of light gossip, but he recognized the note of self-approbation in her voice. He never stopped worrying about failure.

"You said you have a product deficiency?" She nodded. "Why don't you ladies ask your cooks to produce the tarts?" He spoke cautiously, hoping the obvious suggestion didn't insult her.

"We wished to do the work ourselves to show we can manage the whole business on our own."

Such a thought displayed an admirable spirit, but one had to be practical rather than idealistic in business. "I don't produce the goods I sell. I don't believe anyone has questioned me."

"You're a man," Helen retorted. "You could have no employment at all, and yet men would not question your worth."

Nathaniel shook his head, thinking of Winthrop, but he did not want to bring him into the conversation. "I doubt any of your customers are like to inquire much into the origins of the tart so long as the taste is good."

"Perhaps, but that leaves the matter of the stall. Constance was made so ill by the smell of the fish market she still hasn't recovered."

He hadn't intended to involve himself further with Miss Helen Crofton, but he found himself pausing under a lit street lamp. She withdrew her hand as he took out his notebook and a pencil stub from an interior pocket of his coat. "How much money does the society have?"

"Six shillings."

"And the rent at one of the better stalls is how much?"

"Five shillings per market day."

Nathaniel scribbled down her answers. "How many days do you intend to rent it?"

"I'd hoped we could do it in one month."

He refrained from commenting how unlikely it was for them to earn the sum of an indenture that quickly when the market wasn't open more than twice a week. "And your ingredients—how much does it cost you to make one tart?"

"I don't know precisely," she admitted. "I used the ingredients we had in the kitchen."

"You must find out, and that will determine how much you must charge for each slice. You must charge enough that you can make a profit, but not so much that no one will buy." Nathaniel put the pencil and notebook back into his pocket, considering what he was tempted to offer. It was hardly wise to base a financial decision on one surprisingly pleasant conversation and a casual touch of his arm. She might not even accept an offer to invest in her scheme. Hadn't she said she wouldn't take a ha'penny off him?

Still, he felt compelled to try. "I could be your investor and lend you three pounds, and the society could pay me back a percentage each week until you have paid off the loan."

Helen wrinkled her nose, apparently as unwilling to accept help from him as she'd been before. "It will take us longer to earn the money if we have to pay you back with interest."

Nathaniel relaxed a little. That wasn't a rejection of him

but a sound concern regarding the method of finance. "Yes, but you will sell more tarts if you're in a better location." He could hardly believe what he was about to say. "I'll not charge you interest since it's a charitable endeavor."

"How soon would we have to repay you?"

"After you've earned the money to pay off the indenture?" he suggested. Not that it mattered when one repaid a no-interest loan.

Helen's head tilted from side to side. "I'd not planned to seek any assistance . . ."

"It's a sound business practice to make use of every opportunity." Why was he arguing with her? They were almost to David's apartment. He could send her off and avoid her company for the rest of his life. That would be wise.

"Well, you're the expert. I shall have to talk it over with the other ladies, but I venture to say they'll accept."

Helen, naming him an expert? Before Nathaniel could recover from his astonishment, she slid her arm through his again, and they continued on.

When they reached the law office of Josiah Hayes, Helen looked up toward the lit windows of the apartment. "I'd invite you up, but if my sister is ill, I'm not sure we can receive company just now."

"I should get back to work, anyway." Nathaniel pointed in the direction of his warehouse. Helen raised her eyebrows, and he realized it was rather late for business. He hurried to change the subject. "I'll drop off the money soon."

"Thank you, and for the escort. And the conversation." She waved a hand at his coat pockets. "And for helping me clean up the spoils of my transgression."

"I suppose we're conspirators." Despite his serious tone,

he drew a rich laugh from Helen. She seemed to have no difficulty interpreting his wry sense of humor.

"Well, good night." Helen curtsied and turned to go.

Nathaniel watched to make sure Helen made it inside safely with a grin he didn't bother to fight. When the door to the law office closed, he made his way towards his warehouse.

He tried to tell himself he was only doing David a good turn by keeping his sister-in-law happy, but she could've asked David for the three pounds, and her willingness to accept his money made him far more satisfied than it ought.

What had influenced him to help her? He didn't stand to make any money if he wasn't charging her interest. He needed to spend his time working on the plan to bring the tea to market. Unless—could he do both?

Nathaniel's shoulders settled in relief. He could observe all he wished of the market under the guise of checking on his investment in Helen's tart business.

That should've been his primary motive for helping Helen, rather than an emerging sense of altruism. He needed to focus on what was important: the tea and the money. Not Helen's gratifying laugh or the amiable way she'd taken his arm.

He put his head down and walked faster towards his warehouse.

Chapter 7

Helen stood next to Peggy in the Beauforts' kitchen and surveyed her gooseberry tarts with pride. Once the smoke cleared from the apartment, Peggy had insisted on giving Helen baking lessons. "To prevent you burning us all alive in our beds," she'd said.

After five grueling days under the cook's tutelage, Helen had produced eight respectable tarts to sell in the market. Once she wrapped them in clean linen, she loaded them into a large basket and hurried down Market Street.

Though the morning had gone according to plan thus far, her nerves were fraught. What if she'd forgotten something important? What if they had no customers? What if the whole thing was a failure, and she was cast out of the society?

She'd requested a vote on Mr. Carter's offer during their most recent meeting. Constance, eager to escape the clutches of the fish market and still a little starry-eyed about her new hero, had been the first to raise her hand, though all of the members had agreed. Helen had also asked to push back their first market date so she could have more time to perfect her tart recipe. Fortunately, no one seemed to mind the three-day delay as much as she did.

Helen started humming a tune to herself and abruptly stopped when she recognized it for a country ditty about a woman who followed a man to live aboard his ship. She wasn't about to spin fantasies of marrying Nathaniel, no matter how much she'd enjoyed his company the week before. He'd helped clean up the broken vase, which Euphemia thankfully insisted she'd long hated, and walking on the arm of such a handsome man had left Helen embarrassingly giddy for days.

She'd thought he'd equally enjoyed their time together, but he'd sent the three-pound investment by David instead of calling on her to deliver it personally. She'd have welcomed his visit and the opportunity to discuss her amended business plans, but he didn't seem eager to further their acquaintance.

Helen shook her head wryly. It wasn't matters of business that had induced her to take extra care with her hair and gown each day until it was clear Nathaniel wasn't coming. If she didn't behave more sensibly, she'd be in danger of growing as dreamy as Constance.

Jane and Patience had already arrived by the time Helen made it to the right market shed and down the row to the baker's stall.

"Have we had any customers?" Helen asked eagerly.

Patience stifled a yawn." We haven't seen any yet, but it's quite early." Though her hair was neat under her cap, heavy eyelids made it look as if she'd only just woken.

It was important for Helen to inspire a sense of optimism in the other ladies. "Well, let's see what everyone made!" According to the instructions, they'd only made four tarts apiece to her eight—she'd not wanted to overburden them. Helen pulled the towel off one of the tarts to inspect it. "Oh— are those gooseberries?"

"No, we had no more jam, so I had to use dried blue-berries," Jane explained.

They'd agreed on gooseberry tarts so everything would look uniform. "Ah." Helen tried to force a smile.

Jane looked down. "I'll get more jam."

Patience looked from Jane to Helen. "Her father's ware-house was broken into again on Monday."

Helen let in a short gasp. Jane's father owned a valuable property on Dock Street that had already been robbed earlier that month. "How awful! Did he lose everything?"

"The cargo of three different merchants. Nobody wishes to entrust their goods to him any longer." Jane folded her arms tightly around her body. "I forgot all about going to the shop."

And was perhaps short on funds, as well, if her family was in such difficulties. Helen pressed a hand to her forehead. "I neglected to give you the money for ingredients." In truth, she'd decided against reimbursing for ingredients in hopes of paying the loan back faster, but she'd hardly expect Jane's family to donate the jam if they were suffering financial dif-ficulties.

She reached into her pocket and counted out a few shillings from her purse, courtesy of Mr. Carter. "Here, take this." Helen extended the money to Jane.

Jane darted a glance at Patience but accepted the coins. "Thank you."

"I hope your father can resolve things quickly." Helen turned to look over Patience's tarts, all gooseberry and a lovely shade of brown. "Did you make these yourself?"

"Verity," Patience supplied. "She's a wonder in the kitchen!"

"It must be a comfort to come from such a talented family." Helen took a deep breath. "I hope you both read my letter carefully. We must make an effort to be precise in all our interactions with customers so we can develop a good reputation."

Before she could continue with her inspiring speech, a customer walked up to their stall. Helen nearly tripped over their small table in her attempts to approach the woman. "Good day! Would you like to buy a slice of tart?"

The woman, likely a servant by her brown wool bedgown, stared at Helen for a moment and then motioned at the baker. "I'm here for the bread."

"Of course," Helen mumbled. Her cheeks flushed with embarrassment as she stepped back.

Still, they could soon get a new customer, and they needed to be prepared. She started to look for the plates, then recalled Cassandra's words about Helen not delegating. Wishing Cassandra was there to observe her, Helen spoke to her companions. "Jane, will you ready the plates, and Patience, slice one of the tarts?" Patience dutifully pulled one of Jane's tarts closer and lifted a knife.

"Perhaps not that one," Helen whispered. "We'll save the blueberry for when we run out of gooseberry." Patience's eyes widened a little, but she swapped one of Verity's tarts for Jane's without a word.

Jane pulled a few porcelain plates from a basket beneath their feet and placed them on the table next to Patience. Helen frowned. "Oh, I thought I said to bring tin plates, so we didn't run the risk of breaking any crockery."

Patience looked over from slicing the tart. "My mother said she could spare these, as my younger sisters have already broken several in the set."

Helen pursed her lips. She'd spent hours on the plans to ensure everything went smoothly, and if the venture was unsuccessful, she'd be held responsible. Hopefully, broken plates wouldn't ruin everything.

Another customer approached the stall but didn't make eye contact with them. Helen peered up and down the market row. There were many people shopping, but no one showed interest in tarts.

To Helen's relief, Anne Hayes soon arrived with her other four daughters. Aunt Anne admired the tarts and took Helen's hands. "Oh, how lovely! You've arranged everything beautifully. Now, we would like to purchase five slices."

Helen blinked. She'd been through all the dishes at the apartment, but David didn't have a single tin plate in his home, and she'd only asked Jane and Patience to bring two plates apiece. They didn't have enough to serve five people at once.

Temperance pulled the cloth back from one of Jane's tarts. "Oh, is that blueberry? I want that!" Helen closed her eyes for a moment. It was astounding that a person who aspired to be at the top of society would select a less fashionable dessert.

Patience ignored her sister's request and gave out a slice of gooseberry tart to everyone but Verity, Helen's second-to-youngest cousin. Aunt Anne's eyes roved over the table, and then she looked back at her plate.

"Oh, we don't have any utensils. You have to eat with your hands." In Helen's mind, the customers had been perfectly able to pick up the tart and eat it neatly, but instead, the slices fell to pieces when the ladies tried to lift them.

Verity crossed her arms. "I should get at least one slice of my own tart!"

Temperance and Aunt Anne exchanged looks, then started to eat faster.

"You can have mine." Constance passed her plate to Verity. "The memory of my last trip to the market makes me unable to muster an appetite."

Helen winced. Despite all her planning, everything seemed to be going wrong.

Mercy, the youngest Hayes daughter, finished first and returned her plate. "That was very good."

"Yes," agreed Aunt Anne. "Excellent tart!"

Temperance handed back a half-eaten slice. "Quite filling."

They all stood in awkward silence as Verity finished Constance's tart. When she was done, Verity gave the plate back and examined her sticky fingers.

Helen reached into her pocket for a handkerchief to give her cousin just as a man came up behind the family. "Excuse me. I need to get by."

Aunt Anne quickly took Mercy by the hand and motioned her daughters onward. "Well, we wish you the best of luck! Goodbye, dears."

Patience stared at the dirty plates. "How are we to wash them?"

Helen hadn't thought of that. She turned to the baker. "Pardon the interruption, but do you have any water?"

Not even a hint of a smile crossed his face. "Water pump is two rows that direction. If you have a bucket." He was so taciturn that Helen was afraid to ask to borrow any kind of vessel.

"We'll just wipe them clean," she whispered to Jane and Patience and reached for a plate. She started wiping them with some of the linen they were using to cover the tarts. Not knowing what else to do, she threw Temperance's half-eaten piece behind the little table they were using.

To her relief, more customers arrived just after Aunt Anne left. Jane's Quaker friends purchased four slices and even complimented Helen's gooseberry tart. After that, however, they had no customers for hours.

Midday saw the ladies hungry and a little cold from being outside so long. The baker had a little stove where he warmed himself, but the heat didn't extend to where they stood, and he didn't offer to let them come closer.

Jane rubbed her arms. "Perhaps we might take it in turns to walk up and down to warm up a bit?"

Helen agreed; thus, when they had their largest crowd yet, only two ladies were available to take the money, serve the slices of tart, and surreptitiously wipe the plates clean.

"Workers in search of dinner," Patience noted. "Perhaps they will return and bring others at the next market."

Helen's fingers drummed on the table as she considered all the adjustments she needed to make to her plan. "We'll need more plates," she muttered. And utensils, and a system for washing them.

Several of Uncle Josiah's clerks came and made eyes at Patience. "Are you here to make a purchase?" Helen finally asked, goading them into buying slices.

As the ladies distributed the tart, one of the clerks edged to the front of the group. Patience looked pleased to see the handsome young man. "Good afternoon, Owen."

Helen didn't know Owen, but his answering smile conveyed

the purest joy she'd ever beheld. He addressed Patience. "Will we see you later today at the law office?"

Helen glanced from him to her cousin, wondering if Patience had worked up a flirtation with one of her father's clerks.

Patience shook her head sadly. "I doubt it."

Owen looked up and down the market row and then back to Patience. "Will Temperance ever be here selling tarts?"

His eager tone made it clear which of her cousins had captured the young man's heart. Helen's lips turned down. Owen's clothes were neat and clean but made from well-worn homespun rather than fine silk. Temperance would never look twice at him.

"She plans to be, yes." There wasn't an obvious change to Patience's countenance, but Helen thought she detected a downward cast to her cousin's mouth.

"Oh, excellent. Perhaps I'll speak to her then. It's been some time since I've seen her. Years, I think." He rubbed at his neck. "Well, best be back to work. Come on, you lot." He hustled the other young men away from the stall.

Helen tentatively approached Patience, unsure if she'd wish to discuss the conversation with Owen. "Have you known that young man long?"

"Yes, the poor man." After the pitying response, Patience busied herself rearranging the tarts, and Helen let the moment pass.

They got so many customers around the dinner hour that Helen's hopes were raised, but by late afternoon, business had slowed down again, and there were still four gooseberry tarts left.

"Not to worry," Helen told her companions. "We have more

time to sell these."

Jane made a face. "I'm sorry, but I must be home by five."

"It's no matter. Thank you for your assistance." Helen turned to Patience. "I suppose it's just you and I."

Patience shook her head. "I've a lute lesson."

"Oh, well, I'm certain I can manage," Helen lied. She wasn't sure of any such thing, especially not if they had another rush of customers.

The baker just packed up without saying anything at all.

Helen was tired and longed to go home, but she also wanted to sell the rest of the product. Perhaps she should start calling out to shoppers as they did in the meat section of the market. She felt something squish under her foot and realized she was stepping in the discarded pile of half-eaten tart. She ducked out of sight and tried her best to scrape her shoe.

"Are there any pies for sale?"

Helen recognized the voice at once and cringed in embarrassment. How reducing to be found filthy and crouching on the ground. She stood slowly and faced Nathaniel, who was smiling as if happy to see her.

"Oh!" Helen smoothed her apron, though it was too dirty for her efforts to improve its appearance. "Would you like a slice of tart?" She placed a slight emphasis on the last word to remind him they didn't sell pies.

"I—" Nathaniel looked over his shoulder at someone or something Helen couldn't see, then frowned down at her tart. "I'm not much for sweet foods. I'm actually here to examine your books."

Helen didn't wish to infer ill intent from his every word as she'd been guilty of doing in the past, but it was difficult to interpret his refusal to try her food in a positive light. "I'm sorry this isn't to your liking. Wait—my books?"

He glanced back over his shoulder. Did he see another baked good he found more appealing? "I need to ensure my investment is being properly disposed of."

"I wrote down the cost of all our ingredients and the rental on the stall, but I didn't bring those figures with me." Helen hadn't thought three pounds a considerable enough sum to warrant such diligence, but clearly, he took financial matters quite seriously.

He crossed his arms. "You didn't record your sales today?"

"No, but I can tell you how many we sold and show you all the money we took in." Even if she had brought something to write on, she would hardly have had time to record every sale during the dinner rush.

"That will have to do, but in the future, I expect you to record each sale and the corresponding time you made it." His voice rose until he could surely be heard at the far end of the market shed. "I'm always circumspect when it comes to my investments."

He'd no call to yell at her, and certainly not in a public market. Helen withdrew the purse from her pocket and thrust it at him to count. "Perhaps you'd like to take a look at the money? We sold nearly one hundred slices today." Let him find fault with that!

"At what price?" Nathaniel let the pennies fall from one hand back into the purse, seeming to count them with no more than a touch.

"Twopence."

He handed the purse back to her. "Along with my initial investment, you should have three pounds, sixteen shillings, but there are only three pounds, eight shillings here."

"Five shillings went to the baker for the stall, and three to ingredients." She'd not attempt to soften such a cold heart by mentioning Jane's need.

"These are precisely the kinds of transactions you need to record." He shook his head as if he could scarcely credit her incompetence. "You can't trust such important figures to your mind alone."

Did he think her a simpleton? Helen stared at him in disbelief. What a fool she'd been for imagining the two of them could ever be in sympathy with each other.

She was too irritated to meet his eye, and her errant gaze caught Winthrop Morley strutting into view.

It was a sad day when the sight of someone Helen detested as much as Winthrop was a welcome distraction. She turned to Nathaniel. "Do you have any other demands, or would you mind removing yourself in favor of a paying customer?" If Winthrop purchased a slice of tart, she'd never again utter an ill word against him.

Nathaniel looked over at Winthrop. "Oh. I—if you wish." He bowed, then abruptly turned and walked away.

Winthrop approached before Nathaniel was out of sight, pulled his three-cornered hat from his head, and bowed elaborately, nearly touching the ground. "Miss Crofton, how lovely to see you here."

Helen shoved aside her annoyance with Nathaniel so she could smile politely. "Good day, Mr. Morley."

He motioned to the tarts. "I'd no idea Lord David's situation had grown so dire!"

Did he think her family was in need? "Oh—no—this is for charity. The Philadelphia Young Ladies Charitable Society."

Winthrop's eyebrows went up. "You're selling pies to raise

funds?"

Helen inclined her head in affirmation. "Tarts, actually, but yes."

Winthrop looked the way Nathaniel had gone. "Was Mr. Carter here as a customer? I didn't notice him make a purchase."

"He came to see about his investment into this venture." And to make ridiculous ill-mannered demands.

"I see." Winthrop pursed his lips. "I take it you are unaware you must pay a fee to register your business?"

Helen blinked at him. "What fee?"

"One pound." Winthrop drummed his fingers against his hat. "In addition to a five percent tax on all goods sold. If you have the money now, I'll be happy to take it with me.

"Oh, but that is so much, you can't possibly—this money is for a very good cause!"

"Your king's service is the noblest cause of all." He held out a hand.

Helen glanced down the aisle, but even if he would have been willing to come to her assistance, Nathaniel had gone.

With clenched teeth, she pulled her purse from her pocket. Before she could open it, Winthrop grabbed the purse, counted out two pounds, and thrust it back into her hands.

"Wait just a moment!" Helen began, but Winthrop was already turning away. "That's not five percent!"

"Your king has need of it." He bowed again and strolled away.

Helen could only stare after him in shock. Why hadn't Nathaniel ever mentioned a tax?

Perhaps it was only another thing he'd neglected to tell her, along with his bookkeeping expectations. One thing was certain—she wouldn't give him another cause to find fault with her. When next he returned, he'd discover books so meticulously kept even he couldn't find something demeaning to say of them.

She looked around the mostly empty market, cold, tired, and angry, and was forced to admit defeat. As she packed the unsold tarts, she burned with determination to sell twice as much at the next market. Both Winthrop and Nathaniel would discover that Helen Crofton rose to every occasion.

Chapter 8

The following market day, Nathaniel stood in one of the sheds with a brick post at his back, noting the number of people who passed by and musing over his latest problems. Try as he might, he couldn't think of anyone he could ask to stand at the docks the night of the smuggling operation.

"Nathaniel!" David strolled towards him, a little over-dressed for the market in his embroidered waistcoat, but not ostentatious as Winthrop had been.

Nathaniel bowed from the neck in greeting. "What are you doing here?"

David motioned to a stall a little further down. "I'm under assignment from Cassandra to buy up the rest of Helen's tarts for the day before she catches her death from the cold."

"It is turning chilly," Nathaniel agreed. He didn't point out that Helen had a thick wool cloak to keep her warm. From his vantage point, he could see all the activity at the baker's stall, though he didn't think Helen had spotted him, else she'd probably have glared at him between serving customers.

"It's a futile errand, I fear." David released a weary sigh. "Helen insisted upon returning for the Saturday market even though she worked all Wednesday, but I doubt she'll allow me to buy all of her product or be persuaded to leave."

"She's very determined to see this succeed." Nathaniel couldn't fail to be impressed by such an industrious attitude. He was just as dedicated to his employment, and he'd known many men who didn't work half as hard as David described.

"Helen and Cassandra were nearly sold into indenture by an unscrupulous captain when they arrived in Philadelphia. Helen takes the cause very personally."

Nathaniel was surprised to hear the sisters had suffered such a mishap. Perhaps he'd misjudged Helen, and she hadn't led the privileged life he'd assumed. There was likely much more he didn't know about her, but he was just as unlikely to ever discover what those things might be since he'd angered her so at the last market.

He'd been too focused on Winthrop to mark how she bristled at his words until she'd asked him to leave. Upon reflection, he'd realized what a fool he'd been to try and use her to evade Winthrop's scrutiny. He little knew how to assuage her when he couldn't tell her he'd only been making a scene to deflect Winthrop's suspicions without also telling her about the smuggling plan. All it took was one slip, and more than just Nathaniel would be at risk.

If he had his way, he wouldn't have even taken David or Goodwin into his confidence.

He should've taken more care in speaking to Helen. If she'd taken his business advice as censure, she'd likely taken his loud remonstrances about her bookkeeping for Winthrop's benefit as a direct attack. Whatever accord he and Helen shared while walking home from the Goodwins' wouldn't return. It surprised him how much that stung.

For a moment, the two men watched Helen and her companion from a distance. Euphemia Goodwin was talking animatedly while Helen rearranged the tarts laid out before them.

David clapped a hand on Nathaniel's shoulder. "Say—what brings you here? Have you been watching over Helen for me?"

"I'm not here to gawk at women," Nathaniel protested. "I'm mulling over a problem with the shipment."

"Another?" David made a face.

Nathaniel lowered his voice. "The group I hired wants me to travel up the river in the boats, and they want another of my men to meet them at the docks. They believe this will prevent me from being careless and talking about the plan."

"Ah. Who will you ask?"

Nathaniel sighed heavily. "I don't know. Most of my 'men' are day-laborers I hire to move my cargo. I can't be certain they wouldn't sell me out to Morley."

David looked back at Helen. "When do you mean to do it?" His voice was as mild as if he was inquiring about a dinner engagement and not a smuggling attempt.

"November twelfth."

David turned to face Nathaniel. "The governor's ball?"

"Precisely—the one night he should be looking the other direction."

David put a hand on his shoulder. "You can count on me. I'll be there at the docks."

David had a wife and soon a baby as well. He'd made his distaste for smuggling clear. "You'd be putting yourself at risk."

David shrugged one shoulder. "What are friends for?"

Did he consider Nathaniel a friend? "Thank you. I . . ." Nathaniel struggled to find the words to explain how much the offer meant to him. "That's . . ."

"What the devil?" David stalked off suddenly towards Helen and Euphemia. Nathaniel wasn't sure what was going on, but he followed nonetheless.

Winthrop Morley stood in front of the stall with his hand out while Helen counted coins, eyes narrowed in anger.

David marched right up to Winthrop. "What's going on here?"

"Lord David!" Winthrop offered an insincere smile. "I'm collecting an excise."

Nathaniel edged in between David and Winthrop. "There's no excise collected at the market, only a tariff upon goods entering the city."

"New ordinance. Applies to new businesses." Winthrop spread his hands as if to signal there was nothing he could do.

"This is hardly a business!" David exclaimed. "This is a group of young ladies selling pies for charity!"

"Tarts," Helen muttered. She stood behind the table with her arms crossed while Euphemia looked on with wide eyes.

"Do you collect this from all the stalls?" Nathaniel demanded.

"New businesses, yes. Well, good day."

Winthrop turned as if to go, but David stood in his way, arms folded. "I've not heard of any such ordinance being posted. You outstrip your authority."

"I think you'll find I do not. Take it up with the magistrate if you must, though I warn you—he's a great friend of my father's."

David wrinkled his nose in disgust. "I already knew you to

be crass and vulgar, but stealing from a charitable organization under the guise of the law indicates you're without honor."

Winthrop turned puce at the insult. "I'll have satisfaction for that!"

The disagreement seemed to have caught the attention of the market crowd. A few people shopping nearby edged closer to the two men, while the baker who owned the stall leaned forward, not even pretending he wasn't paying attention to every word.

"Name your second," David said coolly as if he answered a challenge to a duel a hundred times a day.

Nathaniel took a step closer to David. Whatever Winthrop answered, Nathaniel would not desert his friend.

Winthrop looked from Nathaniel to the crowd. "You're not worth the risk to my coat." With that, he turned and walked away.

David made a face at Winthrop's retreating back, encased in florid green silk. "I rather think I'd be doing him a favor to put a bullet through such an ugly garment." A few of the onlookers laughed.

"Please don't say anything else," Helen whispered. "You've drawn a crowd, and there will be talk."

David revealed his aristocratic origins with the disdainful stare he leveled at the onlookers. Instantly, the throng turned back to their business. The baker spat and shook his head before returning to stuffing unsold bread into a sack.

David turned back to Helen and crossed his arms. "Is this the first time he's bothered you?"

Helen's shoulders drooped. "He was here Wednesday as well."

Nathaniel had seen that—perhaps he'd even prompted it. In his effort to flee Winthrop's company, Nathaniel had inadvertently led him right to Helen. He'd no notion Winthrop would harass her, else he'd have insisted on staying at her side no matter that she'd asked him to leave.

"That villainous, lecherous—"

"David, please!" Helen insisted.

Euphemia leaned in as if she wanted to hear more. "My father won't allow me to accept even an offer to dance with him. He tried to court me last year, but it was only because I'm a great heiress," Euphemia confided. "What does 'lecherous' mean?"

Helen met Nathaniel's eyes for the first time. "Just that he's like a leach," she lied. "We'll be lucky if we sell anything else today. Perhaps we should pack our tarts and go."

"Wait a moment," David said, forcing himself to turn away from Winthrop's retreating form. "I'm sent to purchase a tart for dinner, and I'm certain Nathaniel also wishes to buy."

"You're certain? I'm not. Nathaniel doesn't care for my cooking." Helen's tone and expression were both cooler than the biting November air.

Nathaniel couldn't recall saying anything of the sort, but he supposed it was more evidence of his inability to speak to a lady. Without a word, he reached into his coat pocket for his coin purse, placed two pence on the table, and turned to go, fearing to say anything that might offend her further.

"Wait," David called after him, but Nathaniel kept walking. David managed to catch up to him. "Why were you so rude to Helen?"

"I believe I offend her by my very manner." What business did a rough sea captain have addressing such a fine lady, in any event?

"I don't think that's it. What did you say about her pie?"

"Tart," Nathaniel corrected. "I told her the truth; I don't much care for desserts."

David groaned. "You rejected what she made. You wounded her!"

Nathaniel gestured weakly back the way they'd come. "At least I gave her money. Isn't that what she's out here for?" He didn't actually believe what he was arguing, but it was better than explaining he was incapable of pleasing Helen and risk revealing how much that pained him.

"I fear that only made things worse." David laid a hand on Nathaniel's shoulder in a fatherly way that was amusing coming from a man so near his age. "You handed her money while scorning her baking."

"Are you advising me to try the tart and pretend to like it?" He could do that. At least, he thought he could.

"Exactly." David beamed at him with a parental sort of pride.

Nathaniel turned to walk back to the stall, but David stopped him with a hand on his arm.

"Not right this moment. It's better to wait until she's calm. Now, should we discuss our plans for the twelfth over a warm drink? I'll try to send Helen home, and then we can be off. "

Nathaniel intended to keep watch at the market for at least another hour. "I have some work to attend to—perhaps tomorrow?"

"Come for dinner," David suggested.

Nathaniel agreed and returned to his post. Further down at the baker's, David appeared to argue with Helen before carrying off two tarts. She did not accompany him. It appeared David's interference had driven her to change her mind about leaving early. Nathaniel couldn't prevent himself from smiling at her determination.

Nathaniel's gaze returned continually to the tart table throughout the next half hour, so he saw when Miss Goodwin left, chattering over her shoulder to Helen until she was out of earshot.

Not many people remained at the market, and no goods had been delivered for hours, but he might still use his time to good account. Despite what David advised about waiting to speak to Helen, it was best to be on good terms with one's business partners, even if they only owed one three pounds. Better not to let another sun set on her irritation.

Nathaniel glanced down at himself. The cuff of one sleeve was starting to unravel, and his shoes needed cleaning. A sad presentation, but there was nothing he could do about his shabby dress at the moment.

His heart pounded unsteadily as he approached the stall. As soon as she noticed him, Helen narrowed her eyes. "I wondered if you would come back. You forgot to review the records." She reached into her pocket and plunked a notebook down on the table. "You'll find it all there—every last transaction."

"Actually, I left without trying any of the tart I paid for." Nathaniel swallowed. If he truly wanted to repair the breach, he needed to make more of an effort. "I was especially hoping to try yours."

Helen's expression softened a little. "Oh." She looked down at the table in front of her. "All of mine have sold, but there are two of Euphemia's here."

At least he wouldn't have to pretend to like it. "Another day, perhaps."

She started to pull out a plate. "You needn't fear to try it; I believe Euphemia helped very little in the preparation, and the Goodwins keep a good cook."

She didn't understand his meaning. "I'd prefer to wait for yours."

Helen's cheeks flushed a delicate pink, like the underside of a shell. Did she think he was flirting with her?

Was he?

"I'll have more next at Wednesday's market." Helen slid the notebook closer to him. "I truly did write everything down, just as you told me."

He started to tell her he was sure all was in order, then realized he'd probably seem even more a fool when he'd been so insistent at their last meeting.

He looked through the book. Helen had a fair, clear hand, but he couldn't seem to make his eyes register the numbers on the page. "You've done very well. Nothing amiss." At least, he presumed that was the case.

A crowd of young men jostled each other to stand in front of the tart table. Helen seemed to recognize them. "Isn't this a little late for the dinner hour?"

A young man edged his way to the front of the group. "Mr. Hayes is arguing an important case tomorrow, and we had to search high and low for a bit of precedent that might help him. Patience only just found it, and here we are."

Helen was already pulling out some plates. "So, six slices?"

Before any of Hayes's clerks could answer, another group of four approached the table. "Oh, I'm sorry—Jane isn't here just now," Helen informed them.

One of the women smiled back at Helen. "We'll still make a purchase."

Helen reached for more plates and started serving slices of

tart as quickly as she could. One of the young men offered her two pennies. Helen looked from the money to the knife in her hand. "Perhaps you can put your money on the table?"

"I'll collect it," Nathaniel offered. One by one, five of the young men paid for a slice, followed by the other four customers. Only one slice of tart remained.

Helen gestured to the young man who'd spoken for the others. "Owen, wasn't it? Don't you want a slice?"

"It looks wonderful, but I'm not very hungry." Owen patted his stomach. "Large dinner."

Two of the clerks eyed Owen in confusion. Nathaniel took in the boy's shoes and clothing, even more threadbare than his own. He probably lacked the coin to pay for the slice.

Helen seemed to draw the same conclusion. "Won't you please let me give you this one? It's very cold, and I wish to go home. You can save it for later when you're not so hungry." She made it sound as if he were doing her a favor. Generous of her and neatly done.

Owen readily agreed. "Of course, if it will help you."

Helen wrapped the last slice in a piece of linen and handed it to him before piling her tart plates into a basket. Within a few minutes, all the customers finished and departed.

"That wasn't easy," Nathaniel remarked.

Helen tilted her head at him. "You found collecting payment difficult?"

He shook his head. "You managed to give that young man the slice of tart without shaming him."

"Thank you." Helen looked down at her basket and then at his face. "I was prepared to argue that you seemed to know how much change to give almost before the customers had their purses out."

"I'm rather adept at counting money." Nathaniel offered her the coins he'd collected.

Helen's hand closed over his, and a sly smile crossed her lips. "You'll forgive me if I count them, just to make sure you haven't made an error."

He smiled back at her. "It's what I would do."

She counted them up and then withdrew her notebook. "And should I record the one I gave away?"

Nathaniel inclined his head. "I'd do that, as well."

Helen made another mark in her book before replacing it in her pocket. "We sold every slice today. Well, all but one. That's a whole pound earned." He refrained from reminding her it would be less after she paid the baker. "And no odious Winthrop to steal from us!" She frowned. "At this rate, it will take us over six months to earn all the money for the indenture."

"You've done very well to turn a profit so quickly after setting out. Your hard work is much to be commended."

Helen smiled at the praise. "I thank you for the compliment."

Nathaniel hesitated, wondering if he should make a suggestion. "If you did wish to increase the rate of return, there is something you could try." He could have kicked himself as soon as the words were out of his mouth. Why risk angering her again? "I'm sorry, I shouldn't—"

"I'm interested to hear what you have to say," she assured him.

He supposed he'd better continue. "Don't take this amiss, but at only eight per tart, your slices are very generous. If you cut each tart into twelve pieces, you'd make more money."

Helen frowned, but the expression seemed more considering than angry. "We—I—wished our customers to be satisfied with the money they spent."

"What about ten? You stand to make an extra shilling for every five tarts." Helen scrunched her face. He was a fool to have risked her good will on so slight a sum. "Admittedly, it's not a very high profit. Eight slices might be better."

"No, it's an excellent idea. I thank you for the suggestion." Helen's smile returned. "You needn't fear to share your insights with me, but if it's all the same to you, I'd rather you not shout or belittle my efforts."

He winced. "My behavior was inexcusable."

"Are you certain?"

She wanted him to proffer an excuse? "I was . . . under a great deal of strain."

Helen frowned in concern. "Is anything amiss with your business?"

"Not exactly," he lied, though he was half tempted to unburden his anxiety about the tea business under the influence of her compassionate gaze.

"Oh." She slid her arm under her basket. "Well, I suppose I should go."

Nathaniel reached for a better explanation of his conduct. "Being an owner continues to challenge me, despite all I've learned. When I make mistakes, I answer to more than just myself. It weighs heavily on me."

"No wonder you miss being a sea captain. I imagine life on board a ship isn't as volatile." She paused. "That can't be right. You face dangers on sea that you'd never see on land. Storms, pirates, mutiny."

Nathaniel chuckled. "Pirates ceased to be a serious concern in our grandfathers' time, and a competent captain doesn't fear a mutiny."

Helen laughed playfully. "Well, storms, then."

"Yes, but you can read the signs to try and avoid them, whereas people are not so straightforward." Though, Governor Morley had always been avaricious. Perhaps Nathaniel had missed the signs that his greed would take a new tack.

"Are we not?" The warmth in Helen's eyes left him with little doubt about her feelings. She looked at him as if she liked what she saw. As if she'd not refuse if he asked to court her despite all her elegance and all his inelegance.

Courting her seemed his best idea in a long while.

She shifted her basket to her other arm. "Well, I'm sure you didn't only come to the market to survey my efforts."

"Oh, no. I had other business here." Business he'd neglected while he circled Helen like a gull. Still, he'd postpone his work a bit longer if she'd allow him to escort her home.

"And I've kept you all this time! My apologies." She curtsied to him. "I won't detain you."

Perhaps she was in a hurry to go somewhere. Nathaniel abandoned his plan to see her to her door. "Good day." He bowed to Helen and watched her leave the market, primarily to ensure Winthrop didn't squirm out of the woodwork and harass her.

A little because he didn't wish to look away.

What was he thinking? He needed to finalize the plans for moving the tea from the market, not to mention to locate a place to hide it the night it was unloaded. He didn't have time to flirt with young ladies.

It wasn't only flirting. Helen was easy to talk to, and for all her grace and beauty, she seemed to like him as well.

He was even starting to think that marriage didn't sound

like such a waste as he'd told David.

Nathaniel frowned at the dimming light. While he'd dallied, the market had emptied. Nathaniel sighed and set off for his warehouse. Musings on marriage would have to keep until his work was done.

Chapter 9

By the time Helen emerged from her room on Sunday, it was half past noon, and she'd missed morning services. She hurried to dress and make her apologies to her sister and brother-in-law.

Helen entered the drawing room and saw David and Cassandra were still dressed in their Sunday finery. Cassandra perched on David's knee while they laughed over something. David had his hand on Cassandra's stomach.

"Do you feel that?" Cassandra beamed at her husband.

David grinned. "My son!"

"Daughter," Cassandra insisted.

Helen took a step back, not wishing to intrude on such a private moment, but the movement caught their attention.

"Good afternoon, lay-abed," David teased. "You missed afternoon services."

Cassandra joined in with her husband. "And you so pious!"

Helen winced from embarrassment, though she knew neither Cassandra nor David intended a severe reproach. "I'm sorry. I was so exhausted from the market yesterday that I was insensible of everything until the noon bells sounded."

Cassandra got to her feet, keeping a hand on David's shoulder for balance. "You should have come home when I sent David to fetch you yesterday."

Helen hadn't allowed David to buy up all the remaining tarts as he'd wanted. "It's hardly an accomplishment to have only our friends and family patronizing the stall."

David raised an eyebrow. "Do you suppose most businesses sell only to perfect strangers?"

"Of course not." Helen stepped further into the room. "I only mean that I might have asked you to contribute the entire cost of the indenture at once rather than go to the trouble of making and selling tarts."

"I still can." David reached into his coat pocket.

Helen raised a hand to stop him. "By successfully executing our plan, I mean to demonstrate my abilities as a leader. Showing up to our society meeting with your gold would only prove I've got a wealthy relation. Besides, you vastly overpaid for the two tarts you purchased yesterday." Ten whole pounds, and he'd refused to accept change, not that Helen would have been able to give him enough back with the few coins in her purse.

David shook his head but withdrew his hand and rested it on Cassandra's back. "One day, you'll have to write down all the rules you live by so I can try to comprehend them."

Cassandra gave David a look. "You're doing a wonderful job, Helen. You should feel very proud."

Helen wasn't sure about feeling proud, but she was relieved the society's plans were beginning to see success. "Thank you."

They all looked up as a knock sounded on the law firm

door downstairs. Westing sped by the open doorway towards the apartment door, just as Helen moved to the window and spied Nathaniel standing on the street. "Did you invite Mr. Carter here?"

David clapped a hand to his chest. "Oh dear, I did invite him to dinner. My apologies, Helen. We have business to discuss."

Helen waved a hand. "No, you must invite whomever you like to your home." In truth, she couldn't regret Nathaniel's appearance after they'd ended the day before in such harmony. Despite stringent efforts to remind herself of all the times he'd left her feeling foolish or irritated, she'd fallen asleep recalling his praise. He'd seemed to truly admire her for convincing Owen to take the last slice of tart, and his words about her efforts with the Society's project had been most affirming. They'd even smiled and bantered like two old friends.

Cassandra's gentle chiding interrupted Helen's thoughts. "Business on a Sunday?"

David laughed nervously. "Well, not really business. More like something I'm helping him with. He's quite early for dinner, however."

"Just through here, sir." Westing had retrieved the visitor.

"I'll ask Peggy to move things along." Cassandra stood and started for the doorway. "Come, Helen, let's leave them to discuss their not-business alone." She winked at David, who cast a hand to his chest.

Helen's heart was in her chest as she linked arms with her sister. Silly, when she'd never reacted that way to Nathaniel's previous visits. Westing closed the apartment door as they stepped into the corridor, Nathaniel a few steps ahead of him. He bowed to the sisters, and they curtsied in exchange.

Helen smiled tentatively, wondering if he'd appear as the grouchy, faultfinding man of business or the affable, helpful gentleman who seemed to admire her.

Nathaniel caught her eye and smiled broadly—freely—as if he didn't care who noticed his regard. Cassandra shifted slightly at Helen's side, and then David came to the drawing room doorway and welcomed his visitor into the room.

Cassandra tugged Helen into her bedroom and closed the door. "What was that about?"

Helen couldn't prevent herself from blushing. "Whatever do you mean?"

"You and Nathaniel, of course, smelling of April and May."

"We don't!" Helen protested. "We were only being friendly."

"Well." Cassandra pressed her lips together, suppressing a laugh. "Perhaps *you'll* be so good as to inquire of Peggy about moving up dinner? And if you should happen to be drawn into the conversation in the drawing room, it will provide an opportunity to strengthen the friendship."

Helen turned to the door. "I'll be happy to go, but I won't interrupt a business meeting." Despite her words, she slowed down in the corridor outside the drawing room and indulged in a spot of eavesdropping.

She was being ridiculous. Did she truly wish to catch Nathaniel's attention by lurking in corridors?

David's strong voice carried easily. "That will do for moving the tea from market to shop, but where will we take it when we get it off the docks if not your warehouse?"

"I haven't worked that out yet," Nathaniel admitted. "I can't approach anyone I've done regular business with in the past for fear it would be too easy to connect them to me. If I can't find something, I might be forced to dig out a smuggler's hold."

"Not much time to accomplish that before the governor's ball," David pointed out.

Nathaniel was a smuggler? Many merchants avoided the duties imposed by Parliament, but Helen raised an eyebrow to hear David hint at his involvement.

"I'm sure I'll find something." Nathaniel sounded more tired than assured.

Helen bit her lip. It sounded as if Nathaniel needed a place to store smuggled tea while Jane's father had space that no one wished to let. Perhaps she could relieve Nathaniel's and Jane's concerns at the same time. But would Nathaniel welcome interference into his business?

She cleared her throat and stepped into the room. Both men got to their feet, but instead of giving Helen another broad smile, Nathaniel's brows knit together at the sight of her.

Helen hurried to explain her presence. "I'm sorry to intrude, but I couldn't help overhearing your conversation. I think I might have the solution to your problem."

Rather than relaxing at the news, Nathaniel's eyes narrowed. "You were listening in on us?"

"I was on my way to ask Peggy about the dinner, and I . . ." She *had* stopped to listen. "Yes. My apologies. It's only that I know of an available warehouse."

"Ah!" David resettled himself on the corner chair, but Nathaniel remained standing, scrutinizing her.

"My friend's father owns a warehouse, but it was robbed twice in the last month, so no one wishes to place their goods there." She wasn't making it sound very appealing.

"I see." David's raised eyebrows made it clear he didn't truly understand why she'd suggest such a place.

"Their family is in very precarious circumstances, and I suspect Mr. Allen would appreciate your custom enough to remain silent about your activities."

Nathaniel shook his head. "I'm not running a charitable institution. Why should I entrust my cargo with a man who has twice been robbed?"

"It would be just one night," David pointed out, "and if no one else wants to use it, the governor wouldn't think to look there. We could hire guards."

"Guards mean more people are aware something is happening, and that means more chance of getting found out." Nathaniel tilted his head towards Helen as if she wasn't standing right there.

"Helen won't spread our business about," David said firmly.

Helen smiled gratefully at David before responding. "Of course I won't!"

David looked intently at her. "You understand how serious the consequences are if this story gets about? The governor means to strip anyone caught smuggling of all their property, and he's already taken a special interest—"

Nathaniel made a noise to interrupt him. "Let her purchase a paper if she wishes to learn more."

Helen's jaw grew tight. Nathaniel might not want her help, but he needn't insult her. "*She* already reads the newspaper. Perhaps you can find a warehouse more to your taste by reading the advertisements." She turned and left the room, forcing herself to walk deliberately rather than run as she was tempted.

"Helen—" David called, but she didn't turn back.

Nathaniel didn't truly esteem her, not if he could dismiss and speak over her so easily. He didn't trust her, either.

Once again, she'd spun a few congenial words from him into a daydream sillier than any her cousin could create. She was a fool.

When Helen returned to her sister's room, Cassandra was stretched out on her bed. "Forgive me, but I couldn't resist a little nap. What did Peggy say of dinner?"

Apparently, Helen was a scatterbrain in addition to an unwanted meddler. "I didn't make it to the kitchen." She turned to complete the errand she'd been sent on in the first place.

"What's wrong?" Cassandra demanded.

Helen spun back to face her sister. "I went into the drawing room, but Nathaniel made it clear my interruption was unwelcome."

Cassandra frowned in sympathy but didn't press Helen to explain further. "I'm sorry. Do you wish David to make him leave?"

"I don't expect David to do that." Still, it would be excessively awkward to take dinner with Nathaniel, and she didn't wish to be trapped in her room for the duration of his visit. "Perhaps I'll pay a call on Euphemia."

"At the dinner hour?"

"She assured me yesterday that my company is welcome at any time."

"Well, if you're sure..." Cassandra pursed her lips in disapproval.

"I am." Sure she never wanted to be within a hundred yards of the confusing captain for as long as she lived.

Helen crept past the drawing room and into the kitchen

where Westing had already informed Peggy of David's guest, collected her cloak, and departed. The previous night's dusting of snow had already been trampled and kicked into dirty piles on either side of the sidewalk. Not unlike Helen's ill-fated regard for Nathaniel.

She'd tried to protect herself from disappointment, but the man had an almost uncanny ability to capture her attention each and every time they met. Helen couldn't quite put her finger on what it was about him that kept roping her in. Yes, he was handsome, but other unmarried men in Philadelphia were quite as pleasing, even if she was too angry to think of any.

His looks weren't the only thing that kept her hoping he'd prove kind and constant. When had any other man noticed her efforts like Nathaniel had with her charitable work? More than notice, really—he seemed to approve of them. To appreciate her as a person, even though she hadn't yet succeeded at the tart scheme.

Not that it mattered. He might admire her hard work, but he didn't trust her, and his behavior was as changeable as a weather vane. Perhaps his humors were out of balance. Just as soon as she could muster the money to repay his loan, she'd bring their association to a permanent end.

The Goodwins' butler admitted Helen and led her to the drawing room without a blink of surprise as if she'd been an anticipated guest. Perhaps he was used to Euphemia's invitations coming to fruition unexpectedly.

Mr. Goodwin alone stood to greet her, but there was no sign of Euphemia. "Ah, are you here to keep company with my daughter? That will be a treat for her. All our other dinner guests are as old as I am."

"Thank you." Helen curtsied, caught between relief to find Mr. Goodwin so sanguine about her arrival and embarrassment she'd inserted herself into a dinner party.

Mr. Goodwin invited her to sit. "Say, do you know ought of this baking business Euphemia keeps going on about?"

Helen blinked at him. "Do you mean the tarts we've been selling for our charitable society?"

"Yes, of course, tarts. Euphemia grows terribly upset with me when I forget that." Mr. Goodwin's expression grew grave. "I must tell you that her insistence on involving herself in the baking has turned my household asunder, and now the finest cook in Philadelphia threatens he'll quit if Euphemia so much as steps into his kitchen again. But does that deter her? No! My once-sweet daughter refuses to consider my discomfort if I were to lose my chef."

"That's terrible." Helen chose not to quibble about chefs, though she knew perfectly well that Peggy was the best cook in the Colonies. "I'm sorry to hear you've been thus affected. Hopefully, we'll earn the money we need before your household falls to pieces."

"Money, is it? Wait here." With that statement, Mr. Goodwin disappeared out of the drawing room, Helen staring after him in confusion.

He returned quickly. "Here are five pounds, my dear. Take this for your Society, and tell Euphemia you don't need her tarts any longer."

They hadn't meant to accept their relatives' donations, and Helen opened her mouth to tell him so in the kindest way she could manage, but Mr. Goodwin cut her off. "No, don't demure. I recognize it's a very generous contribution, but I assure you that I can afford to lose five pounds, no matter how fraught things are with this tea business."

Helen blinked at Mr. Goodwin. "Tea business?" Odd how that subject kept coming up.

Mr. Goodwin made an exasperated noise. "Governor Morley meddles in the sanctity of commerce, and these young men will insist on great feats of daring. Carter will be lucky if he doesn't end up on the bottom of the Delaware along with his tea." Mr. Goodwin froze. "Forget you heard that, my dear."

Helen's first response was indignation that Nathaniel had chosen Mr. Goodwin over herself as a confidant, though if Goodwin was an investor, perhaps necessity prompted the decision. Anger was closely followed by apprehension. "I didn't realize smuggling was quite so risky."

Mr. Goodwin leaned forward as if imparting a confidence. "If caught, a smuggler stands to lose all he owns."

Helen already knew that much from David, but Mr. Goodwin had hinted at more immediate dangers. "Yes, but I believe you said he . . . I mean, do you think a smuggler would be in danger of losing his life?"

Mr. Goodwin folded his arms. "Who's to say? People do odd things when money is involved." He chuckled to himself. "Gold and love. They both have the power to turn a person mad."

Helen couldn't argue with that. The merest hint of affection had turned her quite foolish.

Euphemia burst into the drawing room. "Oh, Helen! I'm so happy you've come."

"Your friend has something to tell you, I believe." Mr. Goodwin gave Helen a very significant look.

Helen eyed her host in return. She could attempt to explain how important it was for the society to earn money without assistance, but Mr. Goodwin was unlikely to respect her position. She ignored her discomfort at accepting his money and turned to her friend. "We've nearly collected all we need to pay off the indenture contract."

"Oh, that's wonderful!" Euphemia exclaimed. "Only I do so love baking and selling the tarts. Please say I can go on helping?"

"What about those watercolor lessons you just started?" Mr. Goodwin quickly interjected. "If I'm to pay for them, I expect you to devote the time to practice."

"Oh." Euphemia's lips turned down for the barest moment. "Of course, Father, you are right as always." She turned to Helen. "My apologies for not being able to help any longer. You mustn't think I don't care about the society or doing charitable work."

"I would never think that," Helen hastened to reassure her.

Euphemia bore Helen off to her room to show off her painting supplies before the other dinner guests arrived. Helen was as responsive as she could manage while thoughts of Nathaniel competed for her attention.

Had Helen judged Nathaniel too harshly? She understood what it was like to be under duress and say things one later regretted. Perhaps she should give him a chance to explain why he'd once again been rude to her.

Or perhaps he'd only ever made an effort to be polite to her because they had a business relationship. Once she returned his three pounds, he might avoid her company or go back to being rude to her all the time. The only way to be certain was to pay him back and see how he responded.

At least Mr. Goodwin's five pounds put her closer to that goal, little as she'd wished to accept it. Of course, she could go ahead and repay Nathaniel, but he'd said that wasn't necessary until the society had earned enough for the indenture contract. Helen wouldn't delay the indentured girl's relief for something as trivial as her personal entanglements.

Nathaniel Carter had already cost her far too much time and attention. She fixed a smile on her face and forced herself to focus on Euphemia.

Chapter 10

Nathaniel threw his shovel down to the floor of his warehouse and shrugged into his coat with some difficulty. Despite a strenuous search, he hadn't managed to find a secure place to store the tea after Matlack's crew delivered it to Philadelphia, leaving him no choice but to modify his own warehouse with a false floor. Three days of digging had left his entire body sore, and his fingers barely able to straighten even when he wasn't holding the handle of his shovel. Blisters formed on the first day of work burst and bled through the scraps of linen he'd wrapped around tender hands.

Digging was long, hard work, but he knew better than to ask David to help with manual labor and couldn't hire someone who might betray him to the governor for a coin. Nathaniel had ignored his growling stomach for hours, but he was forced to stop when his body started shaking from fatigue.

He tramped through the snow to the tavern nearest his warehouse, absently wondering if the weather hampered the flow of customers to Helen's stall. It was a market day, but he hadn't stopped working to attend. He didn't need to observe the market anymore, and Helen certainly wouldn't welcome his appearance. She hadn't even been willing to sit down to dinner with him a few days before.

He'd known at once that his refusal to entrust her with his smuggling plan had offended her, but he couldn't risk revealing any more than she'd already overheard. She didn't have to intend to betray him to give the whole business away. A stray word to a friend or family member might be all it took to bring the governor down on his head. Hadn't one of Helen's cousins maneuvered for the dubious honor of sitting next to Winthrop at Euphemia Goodwin's concert?

It didn't matter how much Nathaniel liked Helen or that David was willing to take her into their confidences. David would lose a lot of money if the tea was confiscated, but Nathaniel would lose everything.

When he arrived at the tavern, the proprietor raised a hand in greeting and brought Nathaniel a bowl of food. Lamb stew wasn't his favorite dish, but he forced himself to choke it down, holding his spoon gingerly with pained fingers.

He looked around the tavern as he ate. Only one other man was sitting by himself. The loner shoveled food into his mouth, never looking up or smiling. Nathaniel looked down at his linen waistcoat and breeches, filthy from digging. He hardly made a better presentation. Even his black wool coat couldn't hide all the mess.

While he choked down gamey stew in a public tavern, David was probably sitting in front of a large fire, laughing with his pretty wife. Nathaniel could almost imagine it, though he'd not had much experience with family life. His uncle had never married, and the men he'd sailed with didn't much prize monogamy. As a boy, Nathaniel had craved the security of wealth, but the idea of returning each night to a cozy home and welcoming wife was growing in appeal. Though a wife and eventually children would come with a new set of worries. Would that be worth having someone always about whom he could trust implicitly and share every fear with?

Even if it was, why would any woman throw her lot in with him? He lived in a one-room apartment above a cobbler's shop. He owned a total of two coats, both dull black.

He could find a new place to live or purchase a new coat, but the one woman he'd ever known who made him question his bachelor's state would probably still detest him.

Nathaniel pushed his empty bowl away and drained a mug of ale. David wouldn't have shared the plan with Helen if he hadn't trusted her. What if Nathaniel had invited Helen to stay and listened to her suggestion?

He might not be sitting alone in a tavern, soiled and sore, eating a stew he didn't care for. He might've gone to the market that day and offered to see Helen home. He might've asked how she felt about courtship.

Nathaniel set the mug down and pushed away from the table. He didn't have time to consider what would never be.

He was back at work when a knock sounded at his warehouse door. His treacherous heart betrayed him by hoping it was Helen. Even a moment's conversation would enliven his flagging spirits and break the relentless strike of the shovel into the packed soil. But what cause would she have to come? It was likely David there to check his progress. Hopefully, he wouldn't be too disappointed that Nathaniel hadn't even finished a quarter of the work.

When Nathaniel opened the door, he didn't see a member of the Beaufort household. Winthrop Morley stood before him, his wine-colored coat drenched in embroidery and a garishly trimmed and cockaded hat tucked under his arm.

Wonderful. The governor's son would be all too happy to carry tales of Nathaniel's preparations to his father, and Nathaniel had opened the door and practically invited Winthrop to observe everything. He was worse than a fool. "What a pleasant surprise."

Winthrop scowled. "I won't insult either of us by pretending to be happy to see you. I'm here for my money."

"Money?" Nathaniel didn't owe Winthrop a cent.

"I was just at the market attempting to collect the excise." Winthrop's nostrils flared. "Those miserly females refused to pay, and as the man associated with the business, you must dispose of the debt."

Did Winthrop speak of Helen's charitable society? Nathaniel made a noise of disgust. "We both know there's no tax."

A cruel smile arose on Winthrop's face. He motioned to Nathaniel's filthy clothing. "Do you mean to bathe and change before you take that up with my father?"

Nathaniel considered Winthrop through narrowed eyes. Much as he loathed the idea, a bribe wasn't out of the question if it delayed Winthrop bringing the constabulary down on him. "What sum is owed?"

Winthrop pursed his lips. "Ten pounds."

Ten was ridiculous, but Nathaniel had to offer Winthrop something to go away. "I'll give you five."

"Fine," Winthrop replied a little too quickly.

"Wait here." Nathaniel shut the door and walked quickly to his office safe. Most of his money was tied up in his business, but he had to have at least five pounds on hand. His hand scraped the bottom of the safe until he found a small, sad purse containing exactly five gold coins.

Nathaniel yanked the door open and thrust the purse at Winthrop. "Five pounds."

Winthrop had the nerve to count them before depositing them inside his coat. "This will do for a start, but I anticipate collecting the other five before too long. Your servant, Carter." Winthrop made a leg, the action mocking for all its elegance.

"I'm certain you will," Nathaniel muttered. He slammed the door. Three days of work were wasted in the space of a few minutes.

Winthrop wouldn't want Nathaniel arrested right away if he expected more money. Still, Nathaniel couldn't expect the macaroni to stay silent for long. He'd lead his father right to Nathaniel's door.

Nathaniel had lost everything.

Chapter 11

Helen looked from the six tarts remaining on their table in front of the baker's stall to her cousin, Constance, who didn't even seem to realize it was past four in the afternoon or care that they hadn't even sold half their stock. Helen hadn't thought the day's snowfall heavy enough to keep customers away from the market, but many shoppers hadn't ventured out, including some of their regular customers.

"We didn't see your father's clerks today."

"Hmm?" Constance turned her face towards Helen, still smiling over whatever daydream had captured her attention.

Helen sighed. "Never mind." Perhaps they'd better give up for the day and hope the weather was better for Saturday's market. There was little chance of selling sixty slices of tart before dark, and her feet were growing numb with the cold.

A loud, large group caught her attention, and she looked to see half a dozen young men pressing toward them, led by Uncle Josiah. They came to a stop in front of the baker's stall.

Helen smiled in relief that they'd sell a few more slices. "Good afternoon, Uncle. And clerks," she added, nodding to them.

"Owen's not a clerk." Uncle Josiah clapped a hand on the young man's shoulder. "He is my apprentice. Best in Philadelphia." The pleasure on Owen's face would have warmed even the coldest heart.

Constance leaned forward eagerly. "Did you win the case, Papa?"

"Yes, and I'm here to treat the young man who worked so diligently to help." Uncle Josiah looked over his shoulder at the four other young men shuffling their feet in the cold weather. "And the clerks, I suppose."

"Patience did a great deal as well. Perhaps we should've asked her along," one of the clerks chimed in. "Um, Miss Hayes, I mean," he added at a quelling look from Uncle Josiah.

"Papa?" Constance's sweet voice softened her father's expression. "Won't you buy up all the rest of our tarts? It's for a worthy cause, and I'm freezing."

Helen eyed Constance in surprised approval. It seemed her cousin had a knack for business after all.

"Well—" Uncle Josiah looked from Constance to the tarts laid out before him. "Of course. Six tarts, then. How much?"

"Five shillings."

Uncle Josiah fished a pound out of his purse and offered it to Helen.

"Oh, Constance—the change." Helen had given Constance her purse earlier when she'd seen Winthrop coming. Winthrop had the effrontery to demand five pounds, and Helen honestly informed him she had no such sum on her.

Constance dutifully handed the purse to Helen just as

Uncle Josiah told Helen to keep the change. "Your mother would be very proud to see you here, my dear."

Unexpected tears pricked Helen's eyes at the thought. "Thank you, Uncle, I—" She broke off, distracted by the surprising weight of the purse her cousin placed in her hand. "Did you sell any slices while I was fetching water?" She hadn't thought so.

"Oh! I nearly forgot. David came and made a donation."

A generous donation, judging by the heft of the purse. Helen's lips formed a tight line, but she didn't complain out loud.

She wrapped the tarts in linen and sent Constance along with Uncle Josiah and the rest. After a glance around the shed to ensure Winthrop wasn't lurking, she ducked down to count the contents of the purse. Twenty-nine pounds. David must have given Constance ten more, even though he knew Helen didn't welcome his interference.

She stood tall, ready to march back to the apartment and return the money. But was that fair to the young indentured girl? The Society only needed twenty-eight pounds—twenty-five for the contract and three for Nathaniel. Why force the girl to wait, potentially for months, while the society toiled away in the cold? The thought of paying off Nathaniel was remarkably appealing, as well. Better to settle her financial affairs before Winthrop returned and tried to take the money away from her.

Helen drummed her fingers on the table in front of her. There was enough daylight remaining for her to finish the business that day. She could send the three pounds with David, as Nathaniel had done to her, but it would be highly satisfying to inform him how quickly she'd found success. She needn't mention that the generous donations came from relations.

David had complained about the smell from Dock Creek in conjunction with Nathaniel's warehouse, and Helen made her way in the general direction, giving the fish market as wide a berth as she could. When she reached a section of large brick warehouses, the first man she asked pointed out Mr. Carter's establishment.

Helen marched past the wagon bay that led directly into the building and knocked on the solitary wooden door at its front. There were no windows on the street level to indicate if Nathaniel was inside.

"Yes?" The voice behind the door was unmistakably Nathaniel's.

He wouldn't even bother to open the door to a visitor? "Helen Crofton here to repay your loan."

The door swung open. "Come in."

She wasn't there to pay a social call. "I just—"

"Come off the street," he interrupted. "Please."

With a sigh, she stepped into the building. He closed the door behind her at once, leaving her to blink in the dim light of a single lantern.

"I have your money," she informed him. "When my eyes adjust to the darkness, I'll count it out for you—all three pounds. We've actually earned all the money we need." The announcement didn't bring the joy she'd imagined.

"You've done very well for yourself. Perhaps you could teach me a thing or two." There was a hint of desperation in his voice. "It's a good thing you've come."

Was he that anxious for three pounds? Helen moved closer to the lantern so she could see to count the coins.

Nathaniel reached a hand out to stop her. "Have a care."

Helen's eyes, newly adjusted to the poor light, made out an assortment of picks and shovels leaning against the wall next to the lantern. He was digging out his warehouse for the smuggled tea. She looked back to Nathaniel quickly. "I'm sorry. I'm not here to pry."

"I don't want you to stumble in the dark." He didn't let go of her arm. "You may look around as much as you like."

"You didn't seem to want me to know very much of your business on Sunday." She hated the note of insecurity in her voice.

"Obviously, it was a wasted effort trying to keep the plan from getting out." Nathaniel sighed heavily. "I'm sure it's too much to ask your forgiveness, but I truly regret upsetting you, especially as it was all for naught."

"Because I've now seen what you're up to?"

"Because Winthrop Morley came not long ago and deduced what I've been doing here, and the bribe I paid him won't keep him silent for long."

Her heart sank. "I'm sorry. I know how much you value your business. What will you do?"

"Is that warehouse you mentioned still available?"

Helen blinked in surprise. "As far as I know." She wasn't sure whether she was gratified he wished to take her suggestion or irritated that his plan had to fail before he'd so much as consider it.

"Would you ever—" He broke off.

Helen shook her head impatiently. Would she ever what?

He finally let go of her arm to swipe his forehead with the back of his hand. Helen followed the motion and noticed both of his hands were wrapped in linen. "Are you injured?"

"I've been shoveling for three days." Nathaniel's voice was wry.

"Oh, now I'm allowed to know the details?" She hoped he could hear the teasing in her voice.

"I'll tell you whatever you wish to know." Nathaniel waved a bandaged hand. "I'll even give you a tour of my warehouse if you like."

"Shall I sign a contract stating to never reveal what I see, or would you prefer some kind of blood pact?"

His laugh was equal parts amused and relieved. "Your word is sufficient. Will you take my arm? I don't wish you to fall."

Helen placed a hand on his coatless arm. The linen of his shirt was soft from repeated washings. "Is your smuggling a result of the Tea Act?"

"Yes," he confirmed. "I'm sure you've read all about it in the paper." He'd remembered her words, had he?

Nathaniel led her forward to the edge of a sizeable trench that spanned the length of the room. Pine boards were neatly stacked against a set of double doors that presumably led to the wagon bay.

She pointed towards the hole in the ground. "I gather you planned to hide tea in there?"

"That was the plan. Hopefully, your friend's father will be able to take possession of it."

Helen voiced the concern that had been plaguing her since she spoke with Mr. Goodwin. "Will smuggling put you in any peril?"

Nathaniel shrugged with nonchalance. "It might be a little dangerous."

Did he value his life so little or his money so greatly? "I

suppose you stand to make a great profit if you succeed."

"Yes, and David also."

Helen frowned. It was difficult to believe David would risk his life and livelihood with a baby coming or that Cassandra would support him engaging in any dangerous activities. "What's David's involvement in your scheme?" Nathaniel looked sideways at her. Apparently, his disclosures were at an end. "You don't have to tell me."

"He's going to stand watch at the docks when I bring the tea up the river."

Helen couldn't determine what was more surprising, that David would take such an active role or that Nathaniel would speak to her about it.

They were silent for a few moments. "I'm sure you want to get on with things. I can furnish Mr. Allen's address before I leave, but let me give you your money first."

"Oh. Of course."

Helen waited in vain for Nathaniel to say anything else before finally handing him three pounds from her purse. "Well, I suppose our business association has come to an end."

Nathaniel shook his head.

Surely, he didn't intend to demand more money? He'd agreed not to charge interest on the loan. "All the money is there! Count it if you don't believe me."

"I believe you. I also recall paying for a slice of tart that I never received."

"You admitted you don't care for sweet foods."

"To be truthful, I've not much experience with them. I can't remember my mother ever making tarts, nor any of the cooks aboard any ship I ever sailed on. Most nights, I buy my supper at an inn or tavern. It's possible I might like them."

She could just make out his smile in the flickering lantern light, but she couldn't do more than stare at him in astonishment. He made his life sound quite bleak. "I'll make a tart especially for you."

"I'd like that." Nathaniel eyed her uncertainly. "Helen, would you ever—" Before he could finish, the lantern flickered and went out, pitching them into darkness.

Without thinking, Helen took a step back, but her back found nothing but air, and she cried out in surprise.

"Careful!" Nathaniel grabbed her arm and pulled her from danger, right against his chest. "Are you hurt?"

"No." Helen's voice emerged as a shocked whisper. The warmth of his body was welcome in the cool of the warehouse, and her heart was racing so quickly she was confident he must feel it also, close as they were. She'd never been held in such a manner.

She found her voice. "What is it you were about to ask me?"

"Have I made myself too disagreeable for you to consider me as a suitor?" His tone was hesitant.

Helen had come to Nathaniel's warehouse to end their involvement, but was that what she truly wanted? "I would certainly consider it." She felt Nathaniel's body relax. "If only I was confident what your manner to me will be the next time we meet," she added.

"I understand." He sighed. "I'm not very good with words, but I promise to attend much more carefully to what I say to you." He paused for a moment. "I—I like you very much."

A warm feeling spread through Helen's chest. "That's good enough to be getting on with, I think."

Nathaniel breathed a loud sigh of relief and moved a

bandaged hand to her shoulder. Helen held her breath. Did he intend to kiss her? She wouldn't mind if he did.

"Come, I have more oil for the lantern in my office."

"Oh." It seemed kissing was not on his mind. Nathaniel steered her around, steps sure in a room he knew well. After guiding her through a doorway, he placed her hand carefully on a piece of furniture—his desk, as it turned out, which she discovered after he'd refilled and relit the lantern.

Nathaniel held up the lantern and smiled. "There, no worse for the . . ." His smile turned into a frown. "I'm an oaf."

"What?"

He waved at her with his free hand. "I've covered you in dirt."

Helen glanced down at her red wool gown. Though it was new that season, it wasn't the finest she owned. The dirt streaked across her apron might never come out, but it was already stained with bits of tart. "Do I look awful?"

"You look as beautiful as ever." He spoke as if making a commonplace observation.

Helen blushed and cleared her throat. "When do you . . . ?" She couldn't seem to string a thought together. "When does the tea . . . ?" Her voice sounded reedy to her ears.

Nathaniel didn't seem to notice anything amiss. "Friday next."

She made the connection immediately. "The governor's ball."

"Yes, exactly." Nathaniel smiled at her, and she returned a grin as if they were co-conspirators.

"I hope you'll be safe." They stared at each other in the glow of the lantern. "I'm sure you wish to be about your business, so I'll leave you now."

"May I see you home?"

Helen immediately refused. "I don't want to interrupt your work."

He was already donning his coat. "It's not an unwelcome interruption." He waved a hand over his filthy clothing. "Though I'll understand if you're too embarrassed to be seen with me."

"I'm not!" she quickly assured him. "Actually, I'm carrying a large sum of money, and I would appreciate an escort." As well as a chance to see if his pleasant manners continued.

Helen retrieved her basket, then Nathaniel pulled open the door and gestured for her to exit first. Even the twilight was brighter than the dim light in the warehouse.

She caught him staring at her as they walked and raised an eyebrow. "I've never seen you in that gown before," he explained.

He'd clearly been paying close attention to her clothing. "Yes, this is new for fall. David insists we mustn't embarrass him by being shabby." She glanced sideways at him. "I mean, not that wearing something old makes one shabby."

Nathaniel examined his plain black coat. Had she offended him? "I suppose you like fine things."

"Sometimes," she admitted. "But I appreciate sturdy wool gowns. And coats," she added. A flush rose in her cheeks. Had that been too bold?

Nathaniel didn't seem to have placed particular import on her words. "I imagine your life here is very different than your life in England."

"Vastly." Helen imbued the word with extra significance. "My parents were kind, good people with modest tastes, and life at Heartcomb revolved around the tenants and the estate production. David, on the other hand, would be happiest entertaining every night and won't settle for less than the finest of everything."

"I'd rather imagined you having a difficult time adapting to living in an apartment when you were used to an estate."

Helen chuckled. "It was harder to share a larger house with five cousins. At least I have my own room now, even if it's small." Nathaniel frowned. "I mean, we were very grateful that our aunt and uncle took us in, and our cousins were lovely to us. Perhaps it doesn't matter where one lives as long as one's housemates are pleasant."

"I see." He nodded. "And is red wool the only color you like?"

"I like black," Helen blurted out, then blushed harder than ever. "And blue, and . . ." Her memory of all other colors had deserted her. "What else do you transport?" she asked quickly to cover her awkwardness. "Besides—oh." Helen looked around, but not many people were out on the street. She'd almost said "tea," but he'd hardly appreciate her drawing attention to that in public.

"Spices, mostly. Sometimes fabric." He grinned. "Not silk, ever since David invested in the Pennsylvania silk trade."

Helen returned his smile, grateful they were back on solid territory. "You're a good friend to him."

"He's the best friend I've ever had," Nathaniel replied matter-of-factly.

Helen's eyes widened in surprise. She'd thought the men no more than professional acquaintances. Was Nathaniel bereft of all connections?

He lingered a moment once they reached the law office. "Will you come inside a moment to get warm?"

"No, I must make myself more presentable and then seek

out your friend's father." He glanced to one of the upper windows. "I shall probably be very busy until all this is over, but when it is, I'd like to call on you."

Helen's heart soared. "I would also like that." She gave Nathaniel Jane's direction, explaining that she didn't know where the warehouse was located but was sure the Allens could direct Nathaniel to find the gentleman of the house. "Well, goodnight."

Nathaniel took her hand and brought it to his lips, no matter they were in full view of the street. "Good night."

Helen nearly floated past the deserted law office and up the stairs. Uncle Josiah must have sent his clerks home for the day.

Cassandra was alone in the drawing room when she entered. Her sister looked up from her embroidery. "Are you just now returning from the market? You must be chilled to the bone."

Helen busied herself unfastening her cloak so she didn't have to meet her sister's eyes. "Yes, I was at the market."

Cassandra's eyes twinkled. "I saw Nathaniel escorting you."

Helen glanced at the window. "Were you spying on me?"

"Perhaps."

"Yes, I returned with him."

Cassandra beamed at the news.

"I don't know why you look so happy about a little walk." Despite her words, Helen couldn't keep a similar expression off her face.

Cassandra continued to smile down at her embroidery. "I think it a very fine thing."

David stepped into the room and frowned at the dirt on Helen's clothing. "Must have been a terrible day at the market."

"It doesn't sound all bad," Cassandra interjected. "Nathaniel escorted Helen home."

David's brows went up. "Was that all right? He was quite abrasive with you on Sunday."

Helen hastened to reassure him. "His manners were pleasing." She didn't suppose David would be soothed to hear Nathaniel had held her close and kissed her hand.

"He has some outstanding qualities, for all he's a little rough around the edges." David sounded as if he was proud. "I've started to drop the odd suggestion of marriage. I'm sure there's a woman who would take him."

Cassandra emitted a strangled laugh. "What about Helen?"

David turned a pair of astonished eyes on his wife. "You think Helen would wish to marry Nathaniel? They don't even like each other very much."

Helen glanced at her sister but said nothing. Nathaniel's interest was so precious and new that she wanted to keep it to herself, if only for a little while.

Cassandra shook her head at David. "I meant that Helen might also appreciate such a kind service. Will you find a husband for her?"

"I've been searching for the last three years."

Cassandra and Helen both looked at David in surprise.

"Far past time I get you off my hands and let another man pay to keep you."

"Three years?" Helen repeated. "You've never said." Why should David have taken such a task on himself when she'd never so much as mentioned a desire to marry? Could it be that he regretted asking her to live with them? "I'd better change out of these dirty things." She left the room before David or Cassandra could say anything else.

Helen leaned against her bedroom door the moment it was closed. Did Cassandra also wish for her to go? It might explain her delight that Nathaniel was taking an interest. Helen didn't relish the thought of being an unwelcome guest. Perhaps the Hayeses would take her back in, though they had a full house already.

She was only being silly; Cassandra didn't want her to go, and David was teasing.

Helen wouldn't allow herself to wonder whether she might quit the Beaufort home for her own establishment. Nathaniel had to survive a smuggling operation, not to mention follow through with courting her. Then they might decide they didn't suit. Thinking about marriage was premature.

She needed to occupy herself with concluding the society's charitable business. At the next meeting, she'd present the ladies with the money, and they'd make plans to pay off the indenture. Everything she planned was coming to fruition. She certainly had the strength of mind not to dwell on a certain sea captain turned merchant turned smuggler.

At least, not very much.

Chapter 12

The day after she'd collected the last of the money needed to pay off the indenture contract, Helen stood before the society and called their meeting to order. Each of the ladies turned politely towards her.

Helen smiled out at the group, which would soon be made just as happy as she was with the good news she had to share. "Is there any new business to discuss?" None would be as important as hers, but it was only polite to ask.

Temperance's hand shot into the air. She'd been uncharacteristically grave since Helen and Cassandra arrived, leading Helen to hope Winthrop had finally lost Temperance's admiration. "Yes, Temperance?"

"I have a consequential matter to lay before you." Temperance's voice was solemn.

Helen had no wish to devote the society's time to any of Temperance's frivolous concerns, but allowing five minutes to their former president wasn't an extreme sacrifice. "Please, enlighten us."

Rather than speak from her seat, Temperance stood in front of the fireplace, positioning herself slightly in front of Helen. Helen pressed her lips together but made no effort to step around her cousin.

"Thank you for indulging your former leader." Temperance nodded to Helen, then turned back to the ladies. "I received a visit yesterday from a very esteemed personage."

Constance spoke in a loud whisper. "From Winthrop Morley!"

Euphemia gasped. "Oh, you poor thing! Did he importune you?"

Temperance drew back in astonishment, more nonplussed than Helen had ever seen her. "What? No, he told me of a terrible wrong." She glanced back at Helen. "I'm sorry to have to tell you that our current president has not managed the financial affairs of this body in accordance with the law."

Shock washed over Helen in a wave. How dared Temperance make such an accusation? She fished into her pocket for the account book. "I've accounted for every single penny we've earned." She'd even gone back to record the reimbursement to Jane. "Take a look for yourself!"

"I'm sure that's all in order, dear, but your bookkeeping is not what I speak of."

Helen gritted her teeth at Temperance's condescension but managed to stay silent.

"Winthrop informed me that you failed to pay all taxes the society owes."

Before Helen could speak, Patience raised a hand, face pinched. "I'm sorry, Helen." She addressed her sister. "I told you there's no such tax."

Temperance returned a forced laugh. "And I told you that

the governor's son knows more about the law than Papa's unofficial clerk." She looked back at the ladies. "We must follow the law."

"An excise on market goods is not the law," Patience ground out.

Helen had allowed the interruption to go on long enough. She stepped around Temperance to the forefront of the body of ladies. "According to Patience, David, and our investor, Mr. Carter, there is no such tax. The only illegality that occurred was when Winthrop stole two pounds from my purse after our first day of sales and another ten shillings after that."

Temperance gaped at Helen. "How dare you accuse Winthrop of theft as if he were nothing more than a petty criminal!"

Helen was sorely tempted to reply that if the cap fit, Winthrop would likely stick a feather in it and mince about in that ridiculous way of his, but stooping to petty insults was undignified. "Perhaps he's only misinformed." She was certain he wasn't, but she needed to mollify Temperance so they could return to the important business.

"I'm sorry to find you so obstinately attached to your own opinion." Temperance shook her head sadly. "I'm afraid the only thing for it is to call for a vote. Which of us thinks we should pay the tax?"

The by-laws forbade any but elected officers from calling for a vote. Helen caught her sister's eye and offered a wordless plea for help.

Cassandra spoke up immediately. "Temperance, what amount does Winthrop say we owe?"

Temperance smiled gratefully at Cassandra as if she thought Helen's own sister would take her side. "He says there's a tax on all new businesses to the market, as well as a five percent tax on all goods sold. I'm certain Helen's admirable records will give us the exact sum."

Admirable records? Helen forced herself to take a deep breath. Temperance didn't seem to intend insult. Could she truly be so blinded by her obsession with Winthrop that she believed his lies?

Euphemia sat up in her chair. "I have no head for sums, but if Winthrop has already had two pounds or more off of Helen, how much more could he expect? It's not as if we've raised two hundred pounds."

"Well, there's a penalty for the delay." Temperance shrugged. "I'm sure Winthrop could explain it all much better. All I know is that we owe five pounds. Now, who believes we should perform our duty to the king and pay the tax?"

"I doubt the king has need of five pounds," Patience muttered. "Most likely Winthrop needs it to cover his gambling debts."

Temperance sniffed but made no reply.

Patience huffed. "All right, everyone, vote."

Temperance raised her hand, but no others went up. "Constance!" Temperance hissed. She gave her sister a significant look, and Constance slowly raised her hand.

Patience made a show of pointing to Temperance and Constance in turn and then tallying the votes on her paper. "And against?" All other hands shot up—even Jane's, though she'd been silent thus far.

"Let's see here." Patience peered at her paper. "Ah, five to two. The motion fails. No false taxes to enrich Winthrop's purse."

Rather than respond in anger as Helen expected, Temperance looked stricken. "What am I to tell Winthrop?"

Helen and Cassandra exchanged another look. Winthrop was a worthless, no-good sot, and while Temperance had a few irritating foibles, she deserved a much better husband.

Jane surprised them all by finally speaking. "Perhaps a man who requires payment in exchange for his attention doesn't deserve an explanation."

Temperance's forehead wrinkled. "But that's not . . . He doesn't . . . ."

Patience patted the seat next to her. "Come, sit." Temperance did as she was bidden without another word. Patience and Constance, on either side of her, each took one of her hands.

Helen collected her wits. "With that business concluded, I have something to announce. Thanks to our hard work, and some generous donations, we have all the money we need to pay off the indenture contract."

Thanks to the unpleasantness with Winthrop, the society's response was far more subdued than Helen had imagined. Most of the ladies smiled, though Temperance stared off into the distance.

Dear Euphemia made an effort. "How wonderful! Should we go right now and free the young lady?"

Jane spoke up again. "Not today. Mr. Morris is away on business for a few weeks, and Mrs. Morris is more likely to cast us out of her home than not."

"A few weeks?" Helen frowned. "You said the situation was dire."

"It is, but if we approach Mrs. Morris and she refuses to sell us the contract, I fear we'll only make things worse for Mary."

Helen's shoulders slumped. They'd worked furiously only to have to wait. "Should we choose another project in the meantime?"

Nobody met her eyes. Helen's chest tightened in worry. Were they tired and desirous of rest, or had her leadership been so poor that they were all hesitant to embark on a new venture with her at the helm?

Cassandra raised a hand. "Perhaps we should consider the matter between now and our next meeting."

"But let's meet sooner than we would normally," Euphemia interjected. "We wouldn't wish to go too long without deciding on a new plan. Perhaps Saturday?"

Helen nodded gratefully at Euphemia's suggestion. "Excellent. Well, I suppose this meeting is adjourned until Saturday."

She approached Temperance while the other ladies perused Aunt Anne's refreshments. "I'm sorry that the vote didn't go the way you wished." In truth, she wasn't, but she was sorry if her cousin's feelings had been wounded.

Temperance rediscovered her commanding smile. "Pray, don't trouble yourself. I'm sure an attachment such as Winthrop and I share can withstand a little disappointment."

Helen wasn't sure what to say when she half wished Winthrop would throw her cousin off for Temperance's own good. "I hope things resolve the way you wish."

She went to stand by her sister, sighing to herself. Now that they'd earned the money they needed to but had no new project for her to plan, all Helen had to look forward to was the governor's ball. While she enjoyed dancing, the situation with Winthrop had the potential to make things awkward. Perhaps if she had the chance, she could inform Governor Morley what his son had been about. Surely the governor could take Winthrop in hand.

Of course, if they all made it through that night, Helen had something else to look forward to after the governor's ball, though she'd not heard a word from or of Nathaniel since he'd escorted her home. She hoped he'd come to meet with David once more before the ball, and she could speak to him for a moment in the drawing room, but she feared he was too focused on his work to pay her any mind.

There was nothing to do but wait. Her unescorted visit to his warehouse to repay the money she owed him had skirted the edge of propriety. She could hardly pay him a social call—if he'd even welcome such an event, distracted as he was over his smuggling plan.

The most she could do to arrange a meeting was to ask David to invite Nathaniel over, something that would surely rouse even David's suspicions about the nature of the relationship. Helen could just tell David, but that rather seemed like something she should discuss with Nathaniel first. She would never be like Temperance, announcing to all and sundry that she planned to marry before any such thing was settled.

Helen accepted a slice of cake from her cousin Verity that tasted much better than the unfortunate slice she'd eaten at Cassandra and David's wedding. She shook her head at the memory. She'd not forgotten the embarrassment of nearly choking to death and having to spit out a mouthful of cake in front of the guests. For the first time, it occurred to her that Nathaniel had been acutely attuned to her distress and had stepped forward to aid her before anyone else. Perhaps he hadn't been so indifferent to her as she'd assumed by his awkward conversation. And then she'd been ungenerous enough to believe he wished to steal refreshments from the party.

All at once, it occurred to Helen that there was one thing she could do to arrange a meeting with Nathaniel. She'd promised to bake him a tart, and David would think nothing of her satisfying a debt if he happened to find out about it.

Cassandra met her eye and tilted her head towards the door, so Helen set her plate down and complimented her young cousin on her baking before taking leave of her aunt. She'd make her finest tart yet, and then find a way to present it to Nathaniel.

Nathaniel stared at the narrow brick townhouse before him. While it wasn't in Society Hill where many of Philadelphia's affluent residents lived, it was nestled in one of the nicer parts of Mulberry Street, close to the center of town. The increased distance from his warehouse would add ten minutes to his walk to and from work, but that would be nothing if the house made his suit more appealing to Helen.

Her visit to his warehouse had removed all doubt from his mind. He wished to court Helen. To marry her, if she'd have him. If her smiles and the way she'd clung to him in the warehouse were anything to go by, she'd consider it. He'd been tempted to kiss her, but though he knew little of courting, he realized an honorable man wouldn't take such a liberty from a woman when he wasn't entirely sure he could provide for her.

He continued to stare at the house without climbing the steps or sounding the knocker. He'd seen an advertisement that the house was to let, but he'd not arranged to meet with the landlord. Everything depended on the tea shipment. If he dispersed it as planned, he could offer a year's rent in advance, as soon as the following week. If he didn't . . .

He pushed the crippling fears away and started towards Market Street, peering into all the shop windows he passed. It had been some time since he'd purchased new clothing, and he wasn't quite sure which tailor would suit his needs. But the only person he could think of to ask for a recommendation would likely turn up his nose at the dark blue wool coat Nathaniel planned to commission.

Eventually, he saw a pair of men dressed in sturdy, respectable garments departing a tailor's shop and ducked inside. The young lady inside the shop was determined to sell Nathaniel a coat of green superfine with silver embellishment, which she assured him was extraordinarily fashionable and would require the merest adjustments to fit him.

Nathaniel eyed her shrewdly. "Another customer didn't pay his bill, I take it?"

She sniffed and didn't meet his eye. "It's a bargain at only five pounds."

He was so aghast at the sum that he nearly turned and walked out of the shop. He had to rally himself to explain that he'd pay no more than two pounds for the simplest coat the shop could muster. A battle of wills ensued over the color, but Nathaniel finally triumphed and asserted his desire for a blue nearly as dark as ink. After he'd waved away all offers of trim and embroidery, she sulkily called for her husband to take Nathaniel's measurements, then informed him in a bored tone that his coat would be ready in two weeks.

Nathaniel hurried away from the shop, determined never

to repeat the experience if he could help it. How did David manage to go through such an ordeal often enough that he rarely appeared twice in the same garment? Perhaps someone as wealthy as David commanded better treatment.

David was already seated in the coffee room of City Tavern when Nathaniel arrived and waved him over. "Well met." He indicated for Nathaniel to take the chair across from him and motioned for a man to bring more coffee. "No tea, I'm afraid."

The servant set a sliced loaf on the table. "Ah, my Sally Lunn bread. Excellent." David scrutinized the contents of a jam jar. "What kind of preserve is this? Not gooseberry, I hope? I've had enough gooseberry to last a lifetime."

Nathaniel snagged the jam after David set it down. "I wasn't certain the city needed another tavern, but I see the appeal of having such large rooms."

"There are more spacious meeting rooms upstairs. Large enough to hold a ball, so I understand, which has brought great joy to my household." David motioned towards the corridor Nathaniel had just quitted. "The subscription room provides all the broadsides, journals, and latest news from England, while the bar room provides all the libations a man can stomach."

Nathaniel spread jam—raspberry, fortunately for David—onto his bread, holding the knife gingerly, so it didn't rub against the healing sores on his hands. "Are you trying to get me to invest in this place?"

David snickered. "No, though I wish I had done when I had the chance." He leaned forward and lowered his voice. "Did you settle things with Mr. Allen?"

Nathaniel had immediately informed David of Winthrop's

interference and the subsequent change of plans. "We've gone over every detail. He'll be on hand himself and will stay the night in the warehouse." The man had been so grateful at the chance for some business that he'd likely have agreed to anything.

"Excellent." David settled back in his chair. "I didn't breathe a word to Helen about any of this, just so you know."

Nathaniel's face was impassive as he considered why Helen hadn't told David of the conversation they'd shared at his warehouse. "Thank you." He wasn't sure how else to respond.

"Happy to be of service. I know how highly you value your privacy." David chuckled. "Oh, this will amuse you— Cassandra took your escorting Helen the other night as evidence you mean to court her. Ridiculous, is it not? I told Cassandra you could barely tolerate her sister."

Nathaniel chuckled woodenly. "Ridiculous." Had David shared that assessment with Helen? Had she believed it? Nathaniel had planned to wait until Saturday night to call on her, but he should visit sooner if she questioned his regard.

Perhaps he was supposed to announce his intentions to David, though Nathaniel felt more than a little foolish explaining he intended to court Helen, providing he wasn't bankrupted. He also wished to make sure Helen wasn't having second thoughts about him. Still, it was hardly the mark of a friend to hide such information, particularly when the lady in question was David's sister-in-law and a member of his household.

David spoke before Nathaniel could. "Back to the business at hand." He kept his voice low, though the other tables seemed engrossed in their own conversations. "I'll escort

Cassandra and Helen to the governor's ball, then slip out. Being seen at the ball will give me the perfect alibi should anyone question my involvement."

"Fighting Winthrop at the market wasn't enough to get your invitation rescinded?"

David smirked. "Nothing short of my being convicted of murder would keep them from inviting the son of an English marquess to their ball. I lend them consequence."

Hopefully, that consequence wouldn't result in David being missed by Governor Morley. "How will Cassandra and Helen get home?"

"I'll go back to pick them up when the tea is settled."

It was as good a plan as any Nathaniel could have arranged. All that remained was to tell David how he truly felt about Helen. "There's just—" He broke off as the men at the other tables got to their feet.

"Sons of Liberty meeting." David pushed away from the table. "Would you care to attend? We are to draft a notice to the captain of the *Polly* that he'll be greeted by the Tar and Feather Committee if he tries to dock in Philadelphia."

"I'll believe it when I witness it with my own eyes." Nathaniel stood to leave. It was hardly the time or place for heartfelt disclosures. "I've more preparations to make."

"As you will." David followed him out into the corridor. "I'll see you in two days."

"Good evening, Beaufort!" Nathaniel recognized Dr. Benjamin Rush addressing his companion. David followed his friend upstairs to the meeting while Nathaniel slipped outside into the cool night.

"Sir, will you buy my last paper?" A thin boy, perhaps ten years old, waved a copy of the *Watchman* at Nathaniel. He'd been even younger when he'd started working on a ship.

He exchanged a few pennies for the paper and turned it in his sore hands, recalling how he'd offended Helen in his zeal to keep his business confidential. He could make a present of the paper to show Helen he valued her intelligence and let her know he far more than tolerated her, no matter what David might have led her to believe.

But was it right to call on her without a word to David? Nathaniel's plan would fall apart without David at the docks. He couldn't risk offending the man by offering a slight.

Nor did he wish Helen to think him insincere. Nathaniel frowned back at City Tavern. He'd told David he had work to do. David might feel Nathaniel had lied to him. He should wait until the next day, speak to David about his regard, then pay a call on Helen.

He started walking towards David's apartment despite his conclusions, hoping the man wouldn't take offense. He hadn't seen Helen in over a week, and he didn't want to wait three more days. He'd just make a brief visit to assure her she wasn't long from his thoughts, then return to his warehouse to go over the details of the plan again.

Chapter 13

Nathaniel's feet slowed as he approached the door to Josiah Hayes's law office, worried he was making a terrible mistake. He might not know much about women, but he was certain men didn't give a newspaper to young ladies they were interested in courting. He really should wait until the next day, not only to speak to David but to find Helen a better present with the little money he had remaining.

He was about to turn away and walk home when the window above him opened.

"Coming in?" Cassandra called down to him.

"Oh, I was just—um, is David home?" He winced. For all he knew, David told her he was going to meet Nathaniel.

"No, but do come up and get warm for a moment."

"I thank you. I—" Nathaniel searched for something to say. He didn't know what he'd even say to Helen if she was even at home.

The door in front of him swung open. Helen, covered in a dusting of flour, was standing on the threshold.

"Good evening. Coming up?" Her welcoming smile reassured him.

"Just for a moment," he managed, following her up the stairs.

Helen glanced down. "Important news in the *Watchman*?"

"I'm not sure. I brought it for you." He thrust the paper at her.

Her eyes sparkled with good humor. "Oh! Thank you."

Cassandra stood at the top of the stairs. She motioned towards a room Nathaniel hadn't entered on previous visits. "Come into the kitchen. It's the warmest room in the house with both fires going."

Helen followed Nathaniel into the room and set the paper down on a shelf, but Cassandra disappeared down the corridor.

Nathaniel didn't have much experience of cookery, but judging by the good smell coming from the oven and the dirty dishes scattered across the wooden worktable, Helen was baking. "I thought you were done with the tart business."

An amused smile played on her lips. "I was making one for you, actually."

Nathaniel smiled broadly. It didn't appear that she was laboring under a misapprehension about his feelings. "Fortunate I stopped by." He took a seat on a stool next to Helen's worktable.

"The tart is cooling now, but it will be ready to taste in a little while. I was planning to deliver it to you tomorrow." Helen plunged a scrap of linen into a bucket of water and used it to wipe off the work table. "I thought you'd be too busy to come around until after your business is concluded." Though they were alone, she dropped her voice to a whisper.

"I didn't want to wait that long to see you."

Helen's smile was well worth the risk of offending David. "How are your hands feeling?"

"Sore." They likely should have healed more after a week without shoveling, but in his attempts to set his warehouse to rights, he hadn't been able to rest them very much.

"I can do something about that." Helen retrieved a large stone basin, filled it with water, and added a few drops from a vial. "Essence of lavender. It works to soothe burns, so I imagine it will work quite well on blisters." She took each of his hands in turn and carefully placed them in the water.

The cool water was instantly soothing. Nathaniel released a breath he hadn't known he'd been holding and smiled gratefully. "Very nice."

Helen returned his smile, beautiful in the flickering firelight. "I think it's safe to cut into the tart." She put a slice onto a plate and brought it to Nathaniel, who started to take his hands out of the water.

"Oh no—leave them. Here." Helen picked up the slice and brought it to his mouth. Nathaniel bit down carefully and chewed slowly, savoring the taste. The gooseberries were a little bitter, but the sauce surrounding them was sweet, and the overall effect was pleasant.

Helen watched him expectantly, and he hastened to swallow. "Very good."

She smiled triumphantly. "I'm glad you like it."

Sitting in David's warm kitchen with Helen feeding him, Nathaniel couldn't remember any time he'd been more content. Is that what David meant about a wife making his life more comfortable? Comfortable didn't quite describe how he felt. "I like the baker even more," he ventured.

"The baker thanks you." She raised the tart again, placing

her free hand on his arm for balance.

Nathaniel leaned forward to take another bite, desperately wishing he knew more of the rules of courtship or had someone to ask. He'd announced his intentions, called on her, and given her a gift. He hadn't meant to kiss her until his affairs were settled, but he didn't wish to cause offense by not kissing her if that was expected.

Helen placed the tart down and regarded him, gaze moving from his lips and back to his eyes. It seemed her thoughts were along the same lines. Without taking his hands out of the basin, Nathaniel leaned towards Helen, and she turned her face up towards him.

The door of the kitchen swung open, revealing David in the doorway. "What the devil is going on here?"

Nathaniel jumped up in surprise, splashing water everywhere. "I was walking by your apartment, and Cassandra asked me to warm myself by the fire."

"You told me you had more preparations to attend to," David retorted. "And you don't live or work anywhere near here."

Helen started to wipe up the splashed water with her apron. "You're home early." Her tone was pleasant.

David shot her a contemptuous look only an aristocrat could muster. "I got here just in time, by the look of things."

Obviously, Nathaniel had clearly erred in coming, especially when the future of his business rested on the man's goodwill. It would be wiser to settle the courtship issue after the tea business was complete, both for the sake of his business and to increase the likelihood David would approve. No man would wish to consign his sister-in-law to a bankrupt man.

He'd make excuses and leave. Nathaniel met Helen's eyes, and she smiled reassuringly.

He couldn't risk offending her one more time. Tea or no, he'd not depart without making his feelings clear. "I want to court Helen."

"I find that a very shocking thing, for you appeared to roundly loathe each other a few days ago." David folded his arms. "If you intend to court Helen, you must go through me."

Helen shook her head. "David!"

Nathaniel wasn't prepared to quibble about David's rules. "Of course." He shook the water off his hands, which had begun to hurt as soon as he'd taken them from the basin. "I should be leaving."

"No!" Cassandra called from the corridor, outside of Nathaniel's eyesight. "Don't go. David, I have something very important to speak to you about."

David whirled around. "What's wrong?"

"I'll tell you in our room."

He flung a hand towards Helen and Nathaniel. "Apparently, I can't leave these two alone." Helen flinched.

Cassandra stepped into the doorway. "They'll be just fine visiting in the drawing room while we talk for a moment."

David considered his wife a moment before bowing in resignation. "I'll be back."

"Come." Helen threaded her arm through Nathaniel's and led him through the doorway.

"Perhaps I really should go." He didn't wish to rile David any further.

"Can't you stay a few minutes longer?"

Nathaniel looked into Helen's brown eyes. David's anger notwithstanding, he couldn't resist such an entreaty. "Lead the way."

Helen settled herself on the couch in the drawing room and invited Nathaniel to do likewise. She hardly supposed they could take up their almost-kiss just they'd left off, not with David tromping about like a medieval knight who needed to protect her honor. Hopefully, Cassandra was taking him to task about that.

She caught sight of a spot of tart dough smeared across her petticoat, just to the left of her apron. "My apologies for receiving you in such a state." Nathaniel wrinkled his forehead. Helen waved a hand at the dough spot. "My gown. I'd no idea it was so filthy." She'd donned an old linen apron, but apparently, that hadn't been enough to shield the blue wool from her baking adventures.

Nathaniel's laugh sounded a little uncomfortable. "I received you in a worse state last week at my warehouse."

Helen laid a hand on his arm. "That was different. You were working!"

"So were you. I've known grown men who didn't work as hard as you did to sell tarts."

Helen's heart soared at the praise. "I'm terribly relieved that we made all the money we needed." Even if most of it had been in the form of donations.

"Did the indentured girl appreciate her freedom?"

"We haven't gotten that far, I'm afraid." Helen smiled sadly. "We're waiting for her master to return to town."

Nathaniel offered her a serious look. "I'll teach you how to negotiate, then."

Not precisely the discussion Helen imagined having with a

suitor, but it certainly couldn't hurt to improve her skills. "Very well."

Nathaniel spoke matter-of-factly. "You must wear a Pennsylvania silk gown and ply him with your baking."

Helen stared at Nathaniel in confusion until the corners of his mouth twitched. "Ah, you're teasing." She smoothed her dirty apron over her lap. Did he think her incapable of learning more?

"I'm not! Such things captivated me." He motioned to her. "You were wearing that same color when we met. Pennsylvania silk. I thought it very fine."

The blue silk Helen wore to Cassandra and David's wedding had been much lighter, but she didn't quibble. "You said it looked expensive if I recall correctly. You declined to say what you thought of the woman wearing it."

Nathaniel winced. "Did I? I thought you very beautiful." He rested his blistered hands, palms up, on his knees. "I should've told you. You're probably rethinking having anything to do with me."

Helen edged closer and touched the unblemished tips of his fingers. "I'm not."

He held her gaze for a moment, then leaned towards her and kissed her, his lips firm and gentle. A whirl of delight swept through her at the sensation.

Nathaniel leaned back against the couch, his wide smile expressing delight without words. "I've wanted to do that since I arrived tonight."

She leaned back and turned her face, so they were eye to eye. "I've wanted you to do that since I came to your warehouse."

"I didn't know if you'd welcome such an advance."

Nathaniel placed an arm around her, careful to keep a loose hold on her shoulder with his injured hand.

Helen gave him a pointed look. "Now you know I would."

Nathaniel grinned and kissed her again, gratifyingly eager, as if he wanted to be close as much as she did.

Sound from the corridor broke them apart, but Nathaniel made no motion to move his arm from around her shoulders.

David and Cassandra entered the drawing room and assumed the corner chair and an upholstered armchair, respectively. David blinked at the sight of Helen and Nathaniel sitting so closely together but made no comment, while Cassandra gave Helen a mischievous look that made it clear she'd soon repay every teasing remark from Helen regarding Dr. Drinker.

David settled his hands on his lap. "We managed to draft the letter, incidentally, and assigned a group of men to present it to Captain Ayers as soon as he docks."

Nathaniel inclined his head. "It seems I should never doubt you."

They couldn't be speaking of the smuggling operation if they intended a group of men to be involved—not unless the plan had changed a great deal since Helen had last heard. "Are we permitted an explanation of what you're talking about?"

Nathaniel offered her a crooked grin. "You're welcome to hear any of my business you like, but David speaks of the Sons of Liberty."

Helen's gaze swiveled to her brother-in-law. "There's no point to not telling you, what with all the loudmouths shouting our business in every tavern. We might as well publish the minutes of our meetings in the paper." David sighed heavily. "We're going to a shipment of East India tea from being unloaded into Pennsylvania. It's a stand against Parliamentary overreach with the Tea Act.

"I don't like it." Cassandra shook her head. "I doubt Governor Morley will appreciate interference with the tea being unloaded. What if you're arrested?"

David reached over and took her hand. "Too many of us for that. We'd fill all the old jail and the new one as well."

Helen wrinkled her nose. "But won't there only be two of you at the docks when you bring in Nathaniel's smuggled tea?" she mused aloud.

David looked at his wife in alarm and then shot Helen an annoyed look. Cassandra only looked resigned and not surprised, as she would if it was her first time hearing the plan. "A man could hardly be arrested for taking a stroll along the canal," David informed Helen.

"Nathaniel won't be allowed to use that excuse if he gets caught with the tea." Helen darted a glance at Nathaniel, who shrugged.

"The men I'll be with on the river know how to avoid detection."

"And he'll have me and my lanterns to signal to him if something goes wrong," David added.

Nathaniel relaxed at Helen's side. "True." His voice was light, but she'd felt some tension depart from his body. Had he feared David was too upset about him courting her to assist him any longer?

Helen tried in vain to think of anything she could do to help. "Perhaps I could stay in the coach and watch for the constabulary? I could whistle to alert you."

It was David, not Nathaniel, who refuted the idea. "Absolutely not."

"I'm not entirely useless," Helen protested. In fact, she was probably quite a bit more resourceful than David, not that she'd be so rude as to say so.

"I'm sure you could manage the business better than either of us," Nathaniel cut in. "But what we need more than anything is for David's departure from the ball to go unnoticed. If you left as well, someone would be sure to remark."

Though she wasn't completely satisfied, Helen couldn't keep from smiling at his words. "We could all leave and say Cassandra wasn't feeling well."

"Then David would lose his alibi," Cassandra pointed out. "We need to make it seem as if he never left."

That would be no mean feat. Governor Morley and his son lived outside the city. Even if David went straight to the docks, signaled to Nathaniel, and came straight back, he'd be gone an hour and a half, if not more. "I'll do my best."

Nathaniel brushed his fingers along her arm. "I'm sure you will." Helen's heart fluttered as their eyes met again. Not many days before, she'd thought Nathaniel despised her, and now he looked at her as if she was the most precious treasure he'd ever seen.

David cleared his throat. "Better not be up too late. Don't want to be too tired for Friday's events. I'll walk you downstairs." He started to rise.

Cassandra stilled David with a hand on his arm. "Helen will see Nathaniel down."

David settled back down in his chair. "Very well. I'll call on you tomorrow at your warehouse so we can discuss any last-minute adjustments. Does ten o'clock suit?"

Nathaniel nodded and got to his feet before offering a hand to Helen. He didn't relinquish her hand as he bowed to

Cassandra and David and led her through the doorway to the front door of the apartment.

Though it was full dark, it wasn't all that late, and Owen Randolph and Uncle Josiah were still hard at work in the law office. They barely looked up from an animated discussion over one of the law books when Helen and Nathaniel walked by.

No one was on the street when Nathaniel shut the door gently behind him. "I just recalled another debt between us."

"Oh?" Helen shivered in the cool air, and Nathaniel wrapped his arms around her.

"The mistletoe at Christmas last year."

Helen sighed at the memory. They'd been caught unaware under a mistletoe ball and had only managed to smash their noses together before Nathaniel stomped off. "You didn't seem to enjoy yourself very much at the party." He'd refused to dance with Euphemia, proclaimed the decorations fire hazards, and decried their games.

"I'm not very much fun at parties." He scrunched his face in discomfort. "I'm sorry I didn't agree to dance with you. I don't know how."

"I didn't ask you!" Helen protested. She'd been frustrated when she thought he was deliberately slighting her friend.

"Are you not fond of dancing?" He sounded almost hopeful.

"I'm quite fond of it, actually."

Nathaniel sighed. "You'll probably have a fine time at the ball, then."

"Not if I have to dance with fools like Winthrop Morley." She swallowed, wondering if she should tell him what was in her heart. Many men favored timidity in a woman, but

Nathaniel knew her true character well enough and seemed to like her for it. "I'd be happier spending the time with you, perhaps teaching you to dance." Perhaps spending time sitting close to each other next to the fire, as well.

"I'd like that." He bent his head to kiss her, then paused to look up and wave to someone in the upstairs window.

Helen groaned. "Not David again!"

"Do you think he'll ever forgive me?"

She rested her forehead against Nathaniel's chest. "Do you think it's any of his business what I do?"

Nathaniel gently tilted her face up. "I can't fault him for caring about you." He kissed her once. "You should go inside and warm up."

Helen, teeth chattering, nodded in agreement. "Will you come to see me when the tea business is complete?"

"Of course." He started to let her go, kissed her once more, and then relinquished her.

Helen walked upstairs in a daze. Little had she known when she woke up that morning that she'd soon share half a dozen kisses with Nathaniel Carter.

David, standing by the window in the drawing room, had his arms crossed when Helen reentered the room. "Helen, what have you done?"

"David—" Cassandra started.

"You turned a once sensible man into a Lothario. I half expected Nathaniel to start spouting sonnets!"

Helen looked toward the ceiling, but she couldn't keep a smile off her face.

Cassandra relaxed when she saw David was only teasing. "Yes, Helen, and it's clear you found his kisses no less distasteful than you do his person."

"I suppose not." Helen didn't mind their ribbing, but she was hardly about to discuss Nathaniel's embraces with the two of them, even if they did spend half their time kissing and caressing each other when they thought she wasn't looking and sometimes even when they knew she was.

David scrutinized her. "I've half a mind to lock you in a tower until Nathaniel gets my permission to court you."

Helen kept her face impassive. "I'd probably enjoy the solitude. I could finally finish that cushion I've been embroidering for you these past three years."

Cassandra came forward and kissed her cheek. "I'm so very happy for you, Helen."

"Thank you." Helen hugged her sister close. "I mean, not that there's anything for you to be happy about. It was only . . ." She wasn't sure what to say about it. Nathaniel wished to court her. He was an honorable man who wouldn't just kiss her and disappear. If things continued to progress, she might be a merchant's wife.

Nathaniel's wife. The thought thrilled her quite as much as it would have shocked her a few weeks before.

Chapter 14

*H*elen walked up the brick steps to Governor Morley's mansion on David's left arm and tried to maintain a peaceful demeanor. Despite both David's and Nathaniel's assurances that all would be well with the tea smuggling, misgivings had plagued her throughout the day.

Casandra, on David's right arm, had been perfectly calm. She gestured to the green color covering the walls in the entryway. "Is that new paint?"

David wrinkled his nose. "That's a very singular shade of green." He spoke in an undertone, though there were half a dozen guests between their party and Governor Morley, who stood at the foot of the stairs greeting his guests before sending them up to the ballroom.

It might be that the candlelight didn't do the color justice, but Helen had to agree that the shade was far too muddy to be pleasing. Perhaps the governor had previously relied on his late wife for decorating advice.

If Governor Morley still mourned her passing the year

before, he managed to disguise it as he greeted the Beaufort-Crofton party. "I'm delighted you chose to spend the evening here when there are so many other pursuits to compete for your attention." He bowed deeply.

Helen's chest grew tight. Other pursuits? She was too much on edge to think clearly. He couldn't possibly know of Nathaniel's plan.

David returned the governor's bow. "I wouldn't have missed it for the world."

Governor Morley inclined his head. "And with your lovely wife at your side, no less. A vision in blue!"

Cassandra curtsied and murmured her thanks.

The governor turned his attention to Helen. "And this beautiful lady in gold. Miss Crofton, you are the jewel of Philadelphia." His compliment was a little contrived, but she made allowances for the older man. "You must promise me a dance."

Helen also curtsied. "It would be my honor." If she could manage it, she'd make sure they danced during David's absence. With the aid of Providence, she could keep the governor's attention occupied so well that he'd not think of David's departure.

Before they entered the ballroom, Helen, Cassandra, and David were announced to the assembled guests. David insisted on securing Cassandra a chair at the edge of the room, though she argued she felt fresh and ready to dance.

"But the baby—" David protested.

Cassandra cut him off. "Will be safe."

"I hate to think of you exhausting yourself."

They were likely to go on in that vein for some time. "Excuse me," Helen interjected. "I see our cousin." She escaped the dispute as quickly as she could.

Patience tapped her foot impatiently from a chair in a far corner but looked up with a smile for Helen.

"Planning to dance?" Helen asked.

"I was dragged here against my will. Papa thinks I'll be a steadying influence on Temperance, but that's a lost cause." She gestured towards the dance floor with a grimace on her face.

Helen turned to observe Temperance and Winthrop with expressions and manners so stately and exaggerated they might have been performing on a stage.

A young man, perhaps sixteen years of age, pushed his way through some of the guests on the side of the dance floor and presented himself to Helen and Patience with a bow. "Excuse me, Patience. I mean, Miss Patience, er—Hayes. Miss Hayes." His cheeks burned red. "Would you care to dance?"

Patience got to her feet. "Thank you, George. I should be delighted." Her long-suffering tone belied her words.

Helen took the chair Patience vacated and amused herself by watching all her acquaintances. Euphemia, dressed and powdered to the peak of fashion, laughed with her dance partner. Constance stumbled over the steps as she daydreamed. Apparently, Cassandra won out in the argument, for David escorted her to the floor in short order. The two made an elegant pair in coordinating shades of blue silk.

Helen would never match Nathaniel in such a way if they married—not unless she wished to dress in unrelieved black. He'd also admitted he didn't dance, though that wasn't such a great hardship as she might have supposed before beginning her new life in the colonies.

She watched her sister and brother-in-law dance and

smiled to think of how much had changed. The third son of a marquess wouldn't have been completely out of Cassandra's reach if they'd remained in England, but with their father's property entailed, true love alone would have convinced such a man to lay aside any chance of bettering his financial position by marrying an heiress.

David said something that made Cassandra throw her hand up to hide a laugh. Thanks to Helen's sister, he was rich in love, and thanks to wise investments, he was growing even more wealthy in gold. And Helen contemplated an attachment to his business partner, a working man, who seemed not only to like her as she was but to relish it. She couldn't know what her parents would think about the match, but she hoped they'd be happy for her.

When their dance was through, David led Cassandra back to her chair, kissed his wife's hand, and made his way towards the exit. Realizing it must be close to the predetermined time, Helen stood to try and position herself near to Governor Morley, who'd entered the ballroom on the tail of his last arriving guests.

He noticed her immediately. "Miss Crofton! Just the person I wished to see. Shall we?" He motioned towards the dancers forming lines. "There's nothing I love better than a country dance."

Helen accepted Governor Morley's arm and allowed herself to be led forward to join the end of the line. Two other dancers separated Helen from Temperance, who stood opposite a young man Helen didn't recognize. Thankfully there was no sign of Winthrop.

It was probably impolite to think uncharitable thoughts about a dance partner's son. She sought a safe topic of conversation to introduce while they waited for the dance to begin. "How is your work of late, sir?"

Her stomach twisted as she realized the foolishness of her question, which could easily lead to remind him of tea smuggling.

Governor Morley smiled wistfully. "It's certainly not easy being governor of Pennsylvania and the Delaware counties in such a political climate, especially as a widower. My home has been bereft of domestic comforts."

Helen dipped her head in sympathy. "My sincere condolences. It must be very difficult for you. And Winthrop."

The governor's smile went from pensive to wry at the mention of his son's name. "I confess I've no idea what to do with him. He needs a mother's guidance, I'm afraid."

Perhaps the late Mrs. Morley had exerted herself on her son's behalf far more than her languid demeanor had suggested. "Ah." Helen wasn't sure how else to respond. She certainly had nothing reassuring to say about Winthrop, and she couldn't think of any widows around the governor's age she might be able to introduce him to.

Governor Morley waved a hand. "But let's not speak of such somber things. You've recovered from your ordeal with the smoke, have you?"

She stared at him for a moment. "Smoke?"

"In the apartment above your uncle's law office?" he prompted.

Helen wrinkled her nose as the memory returned to her. Governor Morley had been with Uncle Josiah when Helen's first tart was burned. How humiliating that he remembered the event nearly a month later. "Yes, we managed to clear the apartment out."

"What a relief." His expression grew serious. "I wish I'd been of more service to you that day. Please let me know if there's any assistance I can render you in the future."

She couldn't think of anything she'd ask him for that she couldn't more readily obtain from David, but she thanked him nonetheless. "You're too good." Helen glanced up the rows of dancers and saw the head couple just clasping hands to begin.

Governor Morley misconstrued Helen's gaze. "Are you looking for your sister?"

Helen didn't dare look at Cassandra in case it prompted Morley to start looking about for David, as well. "I doubt she'll dance again this evening."

Helen was proving awful at subterfuge. Morley's natural response would be to ask why, and if he didn't already know Cassandra was increasing, he might wish to offer congratulations to David.

She needed to distract the governor immediately. "Do you know, perhaps there is a little matter you could help me with?"

"Name it."

Helen's mind cast about for anything she could say. Perhaps the business with Winthrop and the false tax he'd exacted.

Temperance clasped hands with the head man and twirled around in the middle of the line. It wouldn't be wise to speak ill of Winthrop with her so near. "It's a bit of a . . . private matter."

Governor Morley tapped a finger to his lips. "Of course, of course." He opened his mouth to speak further but was forestalled by Helen's turn to participate in the line of dancers.

Once she was safely returned to her spot, the governor stepped forward and bent his head low. "After the dancing, slip outside to that balcony. We shall be perfectly private." He inclined his head towards the nearest set of double doors, barely visible behind a pair of blue velvet curtains.

Helen felt a twinge of apprehension. She only wished to ensure Temperance didn't overhear her speak ill of her cousin's beloved, not seek an assignation with the governor. But surely, he wouldn't think she wished to participate in anything improper? He was a client of her uncle's and friendly enough with David. He seemed genuine in his offer to help her. He wouldn't attempt to seduce her on the balcony just outside the view of his guests. "I thank you."

Governor Morley was an elegant dancer and handsome for a man with a son near her own age. If it hadn't been for her nerves, Helen probably would have enjoyed the dance. When it was over, Governor Morley escorted her to the balcony doors and departed with a wink.

Helen slipped through the doors as soon as the other guests were distracted while lining up for the next dance and then gasped when her eyes adjusted to the darkness. Governor Morley was already on the balcony.

"I didn't mean to startle you, my dear. I came out the other side." He took a few steps towards her. "Now, what is it I can do for you?"

Though nothing about his words suggested nefarious intent, his tone and stance made Helen's skin crawl, and she thought to turn and go back into the ballroom.

She'd already taken up half an hour of the governor's time with the dance. If she could manage another half an hour in conversation, it would be easy enough to cover a final half-hour by insisting David was off playing cards or ensconced somewhere engaged in boring medical talk with Dr. Rush.

"It's about Winthrop," Helen said.

That stopped Governor Morley in his tracks. "Oh, not you as well." He pinched the bridge of his nose. "I've told him repeatedly he must cease dallying with ladies of quality."

Helen could hardly make sense of his words. "What? I didn't—I never—"

"Not that type of trouble, I take it?" The governor's hand fell away from his face. "That's a relief. Did he trifle with one of your servants?"

"It's nothing like that. Winthrop invented a false tax on our charitable society and stole more than five pounds."

The governor placed a hand over his heart. "Five whole pounds!" He pretended to gasp.

Helen stiffened. He was mocking her. "It was quite a lot of money to us."

"I daresay Lord David could return that amount to you."

"Mr. Beaufort," Helen corrected before thinking.

"Of course." The governor stepped even closer to her. "Winthrop's been very wicked, hasn't he? I'd like to get your money back for you, but I'm afraid there's a fee for my assistance."

Helen took a step back. Meeting him alone had been a mistake. "As you said, David could cover the cost. I'll trouble you no longer."

"It's not a large fee." He took hold of Helen's hand and pressed it to his lips. "Only a kiss."

Helen tried to withdraw her hand, but he kept a tight hold on it. She had to say something to get him to release her. "Actually, David might be looking for me now. Best get back to the ballroom."

That seemed to give the governor pause. He released Helen and strode to the balcony door, then poked his head in and looked around.

Helen's stomach dropped. He wouldn't find David there.

What had she done?

Governor Morley turned to face her and pulled the door closed behind himself. "I don't see Lord David in the ballroom." He leveled a calculating look at her. "I don't suppose he's gone off seeking other diversions?"

Helen gave a forced laugh. "He's probably playing whist or some such."

"Funny." The governor sniffed. "He's always eschewed card games in the past."

"Well . . ." What other excuse could she offer?

The door opened behind Mr. Morley, and Cassandra stepped onto the balcony. "Helen, we've been looking all over for you. David just went to see if you'd gone down to order the coach."

"Oh, not leaving so soon, are you?" Morley asked, smooth as glass. As if he'd not just attempted to solicit Helen for a kiss.

"Never before supper," Cassandra assured him. "Come, Helen, let's go and find David and let him know you're well. You know how he worries about you."

"Excuse me." Helen bobbed a curtsy and slipped past the governor.

She and Cassandra didn't say a word until they'd made it down the stairs and out the front door, ostensibly to look at the line of coaches before the house, though David's wouldn't be among them. "Why possessed you to go outside alone with Governor Morley?" Cassandra hissed.

"I thought to distract him with talk of Winthrop and the false excise. He—"

"Did he hurt you?" Cassandra demanded.

"No, but he wanted me to kiss him."

Cassandra made a noise of disgust. "I saw you leave, so I

was watching the doors. When I saw Morley looking about the ballroom, I grew concerned."

"You came at just the right time," Helen acknowledged.

The front door of the mansion opened and disgorged Governor Morley. Had he come to see if David really was outside in search of Helen?

Hoping to avoid a confrontation with the governor, the sisters hastened towards a formal garden on the side of the house. Lanterns made circles of light along a graveled path, which was lined on either side with hedges.

Helen looked over her shoulder. "I don't think he's followed."

"Perhaps we can follow the garden to another entrance?" Cassandra suggested.

Before they could go on, Euphemia Goodwin's voice sounded in the night. "You said there would be dancing bears out here?"

Helen and Cassandra looked down the path to see Winthrop hovering over Euphemia, who had her back pressed against a hedge wall.

"The bears?" Euphemia repeated.

"Let's rest for just a moment," Winthrop suggested. His words were slurred as if he'd had too much punch.

Indignation stirred in Helen. Both of the Morleys were insufferable! She was just about to tromp forward and cast Winthrop to the ground when another figure appeared from the opposite direction Helen and Cassandra had entered the garden from.

"Not again, Winthrop," Governor Morley spat. As he hauled his son away from Euphemia, Cassandra pulled Helen into a shadow. "Miss Goodwin, please go back into the ballroom and assure your father of your health and felicity. He's been quite worried."

"Oh, poor Father!" Euphemia dashed off at once in the direction the governor had come from.

Morley reared on his son. "I told you that Humphrey Goodwin is far too wealthy and powerful for you to harass his daughter."

"She asked me outside," Winthrop protested sullenly.

"Well, that doesn't always mean the lady is inviting you to a dalliance."

Helen's hands formed into fists. How could Governor Morley expect his son to act any better than he did?

"Now, I need you to get to the docks immediately. I've received intelligence that Carter means to bring the smuggled tea in tonight with the help of an accomplice."

Cassandra's fingers tightened on Helen's arms, and Helen had to bite down on her lip to keep from crying out. She was the source of the governor's intelligence. If she hadn't mentioned David, Governor Morley might never have realized he'd left the ball. Why had she taken it on herself to distract him? Her interference had given the whole plan away.

"I have an appointment," Winthrop whined.

"Another assignation? I think not. You'll go to the docks and prove you're not completely worthless."

"Haven't I brought you news of all the would-be smugglers in Philadelphia?"

"All I know is that a common sea captain may already have managed to outwit your feeble mind." Governor Morley's voice was laced with disgust. "I've only myself to blame for letting such a scrawny, sickly child grow to manhood. I should've drowned you as a baby and gotten another child on Letitia, no matter what she wanted."

Even Helen, who found Winthrop completely repugnant,

felt a pang of pity for him. What kind of father would think such a thing, let alone say it aloud to his only child?

Governor Morley backhanded Winthrop, who moaned in pain. "Get moving!"

"I'm going," Winthrop muttered and stomped towards where Helen and Cassandra hid in the shadows. For once, his gait didn't live up to his fine silks and high-heeled pumps.

Cassandra and Helen shrank back even further until their backs were to the hedge wall. Helen didn't even dare breathe as Winthrop passed them, though he never looked up from the ground. Governor Morley returned the way he'd come.

As soon as they were gone, Cassandra let out a heavy sigh. "Come, let's return also. We must act as if all is well and keep making excuses for David."

"Yes," Helen agreed. Though her heart raced, she tried to act calm for her sister's sake. She'd done precisely the opposite of what she should have. All she could do was pray that Winthrop would be too late to catch David and Nathaniel at smuggling.

Chapter 15

Nathaniel took long, steady breaths as he navigated a barge loaded with illegal tea around a particularly sharp bend in the Delaware River. Cruising the river on a barge was a fair bit trickier than steering his larger ship while it was being towed in, and his hands were still tender from digging. Still, it felt good to draw so near to the end of the business.

Unloading the tea onto the rowboats had been relatively easy, though they'd been a little delayed leaving Chester on account of Matlack trying to extort more money from Nathaniel. Eventually, Nathaniel had agreed to ensure the man's silence, and they'd departed. Matlack's crew was as loathsome as the man himself, though that was expected of brigands.

They just needed to make it to the dock, unload the tea, and haul it to Mr. Allen's warehouse, then Nathaniel would pay them and hopefully never cross paths again.

As the rowboat rounded the final bend in the Delaware River, Nathaniel could make out a tiny pinprick of light. He squinted—was he missing the second light? He leaned a little closer.

There was only one lit lantern—the sign for trouble.

His stomach sank. With only one light, the tea could not be unloaded and would have to be dumped in the river.

The smuggling crew knew its business. With barely a sound, tea chests were lowered into the water and released. Nathaniel cut the ropes holding his chests and tipped them into the river with a slight huff.

So much for the plan. His life's work, his dreams of courting Helen—all sunk to the bottom of the Delaware. How could he address any woman without a pound to his name?

The light of a half-moon allowed him to see the others turn back downriver. He should do the same. He'd agreed on the plan with Matlack.

Still, he couldn't help wondering what had gone wrong. Although he couldn't see him, Nathaniel knew David was standing on the dock with the signal. He'd risked life and liberty to help.

Nathaniel couldn't abandon David, no matter what he'd agreed with Matlack. He navigated to a pier further down than the one David stood on, dipping his pole carefully to avoid making a sound. He tied off the barge, pulled himself silently onto the pier, and took slow, careful steps towards David. As he drew nearer, he could see there were two men on the dock.

The grating voice of Winthrop Morley pierced through the air. "I dare not catch a chill by waiting out here any longer. You'll have to come alone." He was drunk enough to slur his words.

"Very well; it appears my friend can't make it."

Winthrop wasn't going to take David anywhere if

Nathaniel could help it. He stepped forward into the light cast by David's lantern. "Sorry I'm late."

"I thought you'd never come," David drawled, lowering the lantern a little.

Winthrop turned and pointed a pistol at Nathaniel, who threw his arms in the air to stop the fool from firing on him.

Winthrop smirked. "I knew I'd find you here. A rat can never escape a trap."

Nathaniel ignored the jibe. "I'd feel more at ease if you put the gun down." He flicked his gaze to David. "I didn't know you'd invited him."

David shrugged. "Some men have not the manners to know where they're not wanted."

"I'll thank you to be silent," Winthrop snapped. He turned to Nathaniel. "My father set me to watch you ever since I learned of your plans to smuggle illegal goods into the city. Imagine how proud he'll be of me when I bring you to him! If you would just call your men in so they can unload the cargo, we'll be on our way to the jail."

"What men? I'm here to meet Mr. Beaufort, so we might take the night air." At that moment, a foul breeze blew past them.

Winthrop took a step forward. "Don't lie to me. Where's the tea?"

Nathaniel feigned innocence. "What tea?"

"You'll not take this from me!" Winthrop growled and advanced towards Nathaniel, stumbling as if intoxicated.

Nathaniel took in a sharp breath and hoped Winthrop wouldn't accidentally set the pistol off.

"I know you're bringing in illegal tea in defiance of my father's order. What else would bring you out here at this time of night? Nobody would take the air here! It's probably rolling with miasmas."

David shuddered and lifted his free hand to cover his nose and mouth. "Very right. This was a terrible idea, Nathaniel, and the last time I'll ever let you set the location of our meetings. Let us be gone at once."

Nathaniel shrugged, hands still in the air. "I'm used to the smell after so many years at sea."

Winthrop made an enraged sound. "Fine, keep your lies. My father will take my word over yours any day, and he's friends with all the judges in Philadelphia. Now, walk slowly towards him." He waved his pistol at David.

"I also have powerful friends," David attempted. "If you let us go, we can all meet with your father tomorrow and settle this like gentlemen."

"We shall settle it with him tonight. He thinks I've no proper occupation, but I'll show my worth." Winthrop laughed, the ridiculous sound incongruous with the seriousness of the situation.

David shook his head. "I really must insist. My wife will be worried if I'm not at home."

Nathaniel's stomach twisted uncomfortably at David's words. He didn't think Winthrop was a threat to them, as long as he didn't accidentally fire off the pistol. He was also nearly certain the governor wouldn't arrest them with no evidence of wrongdoing, if only due to David's lofty position. However, he felt terrible about worrying Cassandra and Helen, and all for nothing, it seemed.

Perhaps he could talk Winthrop into letting David go. "Morley—" Nathaniel began.

Winthrop whipped around. "Silence, you cur! You are

worthless!" He lunged forward and stuck the barrel of the pistol in Nathaniel's face.

Nathaniel's hands shot out to move the barrel upwards. He tried to get the weapon away, but Winthrop only squirmed and twisted, so he couldn't pry it out of his hands.

Suddenly a shot rang out, and Winthrop fell to the ground. David stood over him with the lantern raised in the air. Half the glass was shattered, and the flame sputtered and danced.

Nathaniel tried to catch his breath, mind racing to make sense of what happened. "You struck him?"

"Yes, are you all right?" David crouched down to examine Winthrop.

Nathaniel patted his chest to be sure. "He missed."

"Winthrop breathes." David sounded relieved.

"You should go," Nathaniel encouraged. "That shot might draw attention. I'll see him safe."

"It will be hard for you to move him."

Nathaniel tried to focus his thoughts. "He must have a conveyance nearby."

In mute agreement, they set off together in search of Winthrop's coach, leaving Winthrop himself on the dock. His coach was nearby, easy to identify with his family crest painted on the door.

"Your master is unwell," David called. "We require your assistance to move him."

Winthrop's coachman looped his horse's reins and climbed down to them. While David held the light, Nathaniel and the coachman managed to half-carry, half-drag Winthrop to the coach, and heft him inside. The coachman was none too gentle with his employer's son.

"You'll see him home?" David confirmed.

"Aye," the coachman called, snapping the reins and moving the carriage forward.

David turned. "I must away, and quickly. Come, walk with me; I left my coach back at home." He walked faster than Nathaniel had seen him do before.

They reached Nathaniel's turning. "Thank you," Nathaniel said, the words inadequate for all David had done for him.

"Yes, of course. I'll come to see you tomorrow." David hurried off down the road, carrying the broken lantern.

Nathaniel walked home, going over everything that happened and wondering if he could have done something different.

How had Winthrop known where to find them, and on the night of the ball? He should've been entertaining his father's guests. Was it mere happenstance, or had someone let the plan slip?

Nathaniel groaned aloud. Perhaps that's what became of involving other people in his business. And after tonight, he'd have even fewer people in his life. He'd have to explain to Helen why he could no longer address her, but that was a matter for the next day.

He threw off his coat and shoes as soon as he returned to his small, rented room. He was certain he wouldn't sleep well, but to his surprise, he had barely laid his head upon his pillow before drifting off.

Chapter 16

When two hours passed without David's return, Helen and Cassandra attempted to reassure each other that he was only delayed. Nathaniel might not have departed Chester on time with the tea, or Mr. Allen could have met David and Nathaniel late at his warehouse.

In order not to draw speculation about David's extended absence, Cassandra made her way around the room speaking to everyone she knew, while Helen danced as often as she could and tried not to watch the door. The only positive thing she could say about the evening was that Winthrop didn't return either.

Governor Morley made no attempt to talk to either of them as he circled the room visiting with his other guests. Now that she'd seen his darker side, his friendly disposition to his other guests appeared false to Helen's eyes.

Both sisters were exhausted by midnight. "Should we try to get a ride in someone's coach?" Helen whispered to Cassandra. "Perhaps David is waiting for us at home."

Unlikely, of course, as David would crawl on his hands and knees rather than abandon his pregnant wife, though he might have had been forced to hide from the constabulary and was counting on them to make their own ways home. Cassandra only stared back at her with wide eyes.

Dr. Rush coughed to announce his presence behind the pair. When they turned, he bowed. "Say, I haven't seen Beaufort since the start of the ball. I suppose he was called away on business?"

Helen forced a smile. "Something like that."

"I can offer you a ride home in my coach if that's helpful?"

No response from her sister. Helen silently debated the merits of staying at the ball, making it increasingly clear that David had gone or returning home in hopes he was there. "Thank you; that would be lovely."

"Let us go and thank our host, then," Dr. Rush suggested. He looked around. "Only, he seems to have disappeared also."

Helen followed Dr. Rush's gaze, unsure of what the governor's absence portended. Had he left to meet Winthrop, David, and Nathaniel at the jail? Had he retired when Winthrop returned home empty-handed?

When they settled in the coach, Cassandra leaned her head against Helen's shoulder, and Helen wrapped her arm around her sister. She was forced to make stilted conversation with Dr. Rush, all the while wondering what could have happened to David. What if the men had been arrested due to Winthrop's interference? What if Nathaniel were injured, and David was at his side? The possibilities were endless.

She gently dissuaded Dr. Rush from seeing them upstairs. Even though he was a friend to David, Helen thought it best to obscure the night's activities as much as possible.

"David?" Cassandra called as they entered the apartment. There was no answer. "David?" she tried again.

"He's not here." Westing emerged from the kitchen. "He asked me to wait here until he returned, though he thought it would be before midnight. He left the coach in front of the law office."

"Oh, dear." Cassandra steadied herself against the wall of the corridor.

"I'll go to the river immediately and search the docks." Westing moved past them and down the stairs. Helen wasn't surprised to discover that Westing had been taken into David's confidence. The man would never betray his employer.

David should have sent Westing to the ball. He couldn't have bungled the evening as much as she had.

Cassandra stared after the valet. "Something has happened to David."

Helen placed a hand on her sister's arm. "We don't know that. There might be any number of explanations for why he's not here. Now come and change out of your gown."

She led her sister into her bedroom and helped her undress like she had when they were children. Helen suggested Cassandra lie down, but the proposal was met by a glare.

"Give me that," Cassandra said, reaching for David's wrapper. She slid her arms in and cinched the belt above her rounded belly tightly as if securing his wrapper would anchor him to her.

They sat in the drawing room until the sun rose, but there was no sign of David or Westing.

"Perhaps Westing is assisting David with something?" Helen suggested weakly. Cassandra only buried her face in her hands.

Helen stood from the couch. She'd go to Mr. Allen's warehouse. She should've told Westing to try there. She hadn't bothered to change out of her finery and would undoubtedly draw attention on Dock Street, but she couldn't waste time. "I'll be back soon. Try not to fret, dearest. All will be well."

Before she could leave, a knock sounded at the door. Helen raced to open it, all the while knowing that David or Westing would have just come in. But Nathaniel would knock.

Uncle Josiah stood on the other side of the door, a grave expression on his face. As he stepped inside, Helen blurted out, "We can't find David!" Her uncle was a lawyer. If David was in legal trouble, he could find no one better poised to assist him.

"I know where he is."

Cassandra emerged into the corridor, stumbling in her haste. "Where? Is he hurt?"

"He is uninjured." Uncle Josiah gestured towards the drawing room. "We should sit." Helen and Cassandra obediently followed him down the corridor. Helen sat down on the couch by Cassandra and took her hand.

Uncle Josiah offered them a tight smile. "I received a missive this morning from David. He was taken into custody late last night."

Helen drew in a sharp breath. "For what?"

"Murder."

Cassandra threw a hand over her mouth. "What! Who's died?"

"Winthrop Morley." Uncle Josiah's voice was grave. "I don't know much more. I should be allowed to see David so I can provide legal guidance."

"Why did he not write to *me*?" Cassandra's voice was barely more than a whisper.

"Perhaps he didn't wish to alarm you?"

Cassandra stared at their uncle in disbelief. "He didn't think I'd be more worried when he never returned?"

Uncle Josiah could only shrug.

"Was anyone else arrested?" Helen asked, thinking of Nathaniel.

"Not that David mentioned in his letter." Uncle Josiah stood. "I'd better go to him now. I'll be back as soon as I know anything."

Cassandra's hand shot out and grabbed his. "Please, Uncle—this must be a mistake. You must sort everything out and bring him back to me. David would never . . ."

"I'll do everything I can," he assured her, patting her hand.

Helen turned to her sister and took in her pale, exhausted face. "Cassandra, *please* lie down. You look as if you're about to faint. Remember the baby."

Cassandra cradled her stomach with her hands. "All right."

Once she'd gotten Cassandra settled in bed, Helen paced the drawing room. David, jailed for murder? And no mention of Nathaniel. Wouldn't David have mentioned if his friend needed legal advice as well?

Not knowing was insufferable. Helen didn't know where Nathaniel lived, but she could check his warehouse.

After ensuring Cassandra slept, Helen set off at once, feeling increasingly wretched. If she hadn't tried to distract Morley, he wouldn't have sent Winthrop off to confront David—and apparently, to die. It hardly seemed possible that a man she'd seen alive and well a few hours before could be dead.

Whatever had happened, David wasn't responsible for Winthrop's death.

She quickened her pace. Hopefully, Nathaniel would have some answers. Something to comfort her, if only the sanctuary of his arms.

Nathaniel woke to the sound of someone pounding on his door. David had said he'd come the next day, but it was unlike him to be such an early riser.

"One moment," he called through the door as he pulled his breeches on.

"It's me—Helen."

Helen? Something must be terribly wrong for her to show up at his room. He hastened to pull on his clothing and opened his door before he'd finished the top buttons on his waistcoat. "What's happened?"

Helen was dressed in an elaborate gown, but it was wrinkled, and several strands of hair were displaced from her coiffure. "David's been arrested."

"Arrested?" Nathaniel repeated. Why would Winthrop have roused the constabulary against David and not him? He hurried to fasten the rest of the buttons. "For smuggling?"

"For Winthrop Morley's murder."

Nathaniel froze with a hand still reaching for his coat. "Winthrop is dead?"

Helen shrugged helplessly. "According to my uncle. David sent him a letter from jail."

They heard voices on the stair, and Nathaniel motioned

for Helen to come inside. If the cobbler's nosy wife knew he had a woman in his room, she'd do more than raise an eyebrow. Best to keep Helen's presence a secret.

She accepted his offer of the room's lone chair. "Tell me what happened last night," Helen begged.

Nathaniel related the experience of the previous night. "Winthrop was still alive when we put him in that coach."

"But you said David struck him with a lantern?" Helen breathed. "Oh, how could he?"

"Winthrop was about to shoot me," Nathaniel admitted. "This is all my fault." He shouldn't have let a man with a wife and baby on the way involve himself.

"No," Helen said vehemently. "This is *my* fault."

Suspicion rose in Nathaniel, though he tried to quash it. "You didn't tell Winthrop where to find us, did you?"

"Not Winthrop. His father."

"You told the governor we were moving illegal tea?" Not in his wildest imagination could Nathaniel have dreamt Helen would betray him like that, not to mention her brother-in-law.

"Not on purpose!" Helen moaned. "I thought to distract the governor's attention from David's departure, so I danced with him and then tried to speak with him about Winthrop's false tax. He took me wanting to meet with him as . . ." Her voice trailed off. "He tried to . . ."

Nathaniel took a step towards Helen. "What?" If Morley had so much as touched her, Nathaniel would tear him limb from limb.

"He wanted to kiss me." Helen seemed unable to meet his eyes. "I wanted to get away from him. I wasn't thinking properly. I told him that David would be looking for me, which made him look about and discover David had gone. Then governor sent

Winthrop after you."

Nathaniel clenched his fists. Helen had gone to Morley for help about his wretched son, and he'd tried to corner her for a kiss? "I suppose you could do no less than remind him of David." The governor would be a fool to insult the sister-in-law of such a wealthy and powerful man.

"I'm sorry." Helen's voice broke. "If David hangs for murder and it's all my fault—"

Nathaniel would give anything to bring her relief. "He won't," he interrupted. "It was my tea and my plan. I'm going to go to the magistrate now and offer to take his place."

Helen stood and closed the distance between them. "What if they keep you but refuse to let David go?"

Nathaniel clutched her elbows. "David has a wife and baby on the way. It's worth the risk." He had no one.

Tears welled up in Helen's brown eyes. He started to move his hands to wipe them away but stopped himself just in time. "Helen, I lost everything last night. Everything left will have to be sold to appease the creditors, and even then, it might not be enough." He had nothing to offer her.

"I'm so very sorry." Her voice was earnest, heartfelt. Nathaniel's heart thrummed painfully as he contemplated the future they'd never have.

She stepped away from him. "I'm sure you won't wish to come to the apartment, even if you're not able to take David's place. I hope you know I wish you well."

He stared at her in confusion. Did she mean never to see him again?

Perhaps it was for the best. Being in one another's company could only be a painful reminder of their loss. "I understand."

She nodded once, then curtsied. "Good day."

A few weeks before Nathaniel had insisted he didn't need a wife, and it wasn't as if he and Helen were engaged, or even publicly courting. Why then did his chest grow tight as she left?

He forced himself to breathe, in and out. He didn't have time to feel sorry for himself while David festered in jail.

Nathaniel buckled his shoes and departed mere minutes after Helen. He walked without knowing quite where he was going. There was more than one magistrate in the city, and he'd no way of identifying which one had taken David's case, nor what he should say if he could find the correct one.

If he confessed to smuggling, he'd forfeit all his business and property, along with any chance to pay back even a portion of what he owed his creditors—including David. If Nathaniel said he'd been the one to strike Winthrop, he could well hang for murder, and as Helen said, they could decide to keep David as well. Confessing could make things worse, but so could staying silent.

His head ached as he turned the problem over in his mind, wishing there was someone he could talk the matter over with. He'd lost all right to Helen's company, and David was in jail, all because Nathaniel hadn't trusted his instinct not to allow a man with a family to do something dangerous.

Nathaniel passed City Tavern, wincing at the memory of meeting David there. David was the only friend he had, and he'd ruined the man's life.

A shout from someone on the street interrupted his circling thoughts. "You!"

Nathaniel turned to see Governor Morley standing on Second Street glaring at him. Nathaniel could continue on his way but hearing what the man said might prove valuable. At the very least, Nathaniel should offer condolences, no matter what he'd thought of Winthrop.

Nathaniel approached the man and bowed. "I was very sorry to hear of your loss."

Morley's scowl deepened. "Sorry but not surprised, I daresay, as you participated in his murder, for all Beaufort seeks to protect you."

He opened his mouth to tell Morley what had actually happened but stopped himself. David might have an inscrutable reason for obscuring Nathaniel's presence at the docks. "I know not what you mean, sir. I could not have been more astonished at the news." Especially as he'd seen Winthrop very much alive when they'd parted company.

"I know better than to credit the word of a smuggler." Morley's mirthless laugh was chilling. "Don't think I'll rest until I see you and Beaufort hanged along with your goods seized. I intend to avenge my son."

Nathaniel ignored the threat to his life, more concerned the governor meant to go after David for smuggling as well. If the worst happened, David's surviving family wouldn't be able to live without any money. "Allow me to assure you that no smuggling took place." It wasn't a lie; the tea hadn't even been unloaded onto Philadelphia land.

"You'll forgive me for not believing that. Well, enjoy your freedom, Mr. Carter. This may well be your last opportunity." Morley strode away without taking any leave.

Nathaniel had taken steps to obscure his business, but he'd make doubly sure there was no evidence for the governor to find, nor anything that could connect David to him other than being a friend and investor. Nathaniel would also have to warn

Humphrey Goodwin not to talk or risk being swept up himself.

Once the secret was assured, Nathaniel could turn his attentions back to finding the magistrate and determining the best story to give so David could go free. It was the least Nathaniel could do, but he had nothing else to offer and only himself to blame for their misfortunes.

Chapter 17

*H*elen barely managed to hold back the tears as she walked back to her sister. All of Nathaniel's respect for her, gone, and it was entirely her fault. Why had she meddled in his plan? All she'd needed to do was attend the party and deflect questions about David. Instead, she'd taken it upon herself to distract the governor. Nathaniel had been right to fear trusting her with his secret.

No matter how much his anger hurt, she couldn't blame him. Everything he'd worked for in life, gone in a few hours. And still, he'd done no more than clench his fists when she'd confessed the truth. He hadn't yelled at her or reminded her how he'd worked his way from humble circumstances to be the owner of three ships, now lost due to her stupidity. His voice had been kind, even sad, when he told her he'd lost everything.

If he regretted the end of their association, it was so much the worse for both of them. No man would want a wife who'd lost him his livelihood.

She took a deep breath before opening the door to the law office. Cassandra mustn't be troubled by any of Helen's problems. She tried to hold a serene expression.

There was no sign of Uncle Josiah, but the clerks eyed Helen as if they'd heard something was amiss with the tenants upstairs. Owen Randolph even smiled sympathetically.

Westing was coming out of the drawing room when Helen entered the apartment. "Oh, you're back."

"I tracked Mr. Beaufort to the jail, but they won't let me stay with him, so I returned here." Westing shook his head sadly. "I'm afraid I can't tempt Mrs. Beaufort to eat, but perhaps you'll have better luck." He spoke as calmly as ever, but there was sadness in his eyes.

Helen was sure that if allowed, Westing would trade places with David at the jail without a second thought. "Thank you, Westing. You're always good to us."

Cassandra was pacing when Helen came in. As soon as she saw the latest arrival wasn't David, Cassandra resumed treading the floorboards. "Oh, when will Uncle return with news?" Her eyes darted to the mantel clock.

"It might take a little while to sort things out, dearest, but I know he'll be back. Now, won't you sip this broth?" Helen lifted the bowl Westing had left.

Cassandra shook her head. "I can't eat. The very notion makes me ill."

In vain, Helen tried to get her to take even a sip of broth. Not even arguments about the health of the baby could induce Cassandra's rolling stomach to attempt it.

Throughout the day, the wait seemed unbearable. Neither sister could focus her mind on any occupation. Helen debated telling Cassandra what she'd heard from Nathaniel, but nothing he'd said revealed more than her sister already knew, and she feared displaying too much of her own sadness if she opened the topic.

At mid-afternoon, they heard a knock at the door. Helen sprang up to answer it, but Cassandra pushed past her to fling it open. Her face fell when she saw only their Aunt and Uncle Hayes, unaccompanied by David.

"He's not free yet?"

Uncle Josiah placed a steadying hand under Cassandra's elbow. "Come and sit, and I'll tell you all I know."

Helen once more held Cassandra's hand on the couch while their aunt and uncle sat in chairs across from them.

"I was able to see David," Uncle Josiah began.

Cassandra nearly sprang from the couch. "How is he?" Helen gently tugged her sister back to her seat.

"He's as well as he could be, considering the circumstances," Uncle Josiah assured them. "It seems last evening he met a friend at the docks, and some kind of fight broke out. Winthrop Morley was knocked down and died as a result of the blow."

Cassandra drew back at the news. "What evidence do they have that my husband was involved?"

Uncle Josiah sighed. "The word of the governor."

"I'm not sure how he could have anything to say about the matter when he was at the ball all night," Helen retorted. But that wasn't true—Dr. Rush hadn't been able to locate their host when they'd left.

"According to Governor Morley, he stepped away from the ball for a moment and found a note from Winthrop indicating he'd left to apprehend smugglers. Governor Morley grew concerned when Winthrop didn't ever return and rode out to look for him."

Helen and Cassandra exchanged a quick look. They knew for a fact that the governor hadn't received any such note, but Helen wasn't sure if they should tell their uncle—or their aunt—any more about the smuggling plan.

"And my husband?" Cassandra pressed.

"The governor apprehended his own coach and found Winthrop dead inside. He questioned his driver, who described the two men who allegedly assaulted Winthrop before delivering him to his own coach. Based on the coachman's description, Governor Morley identified David, located him on the street not far from this apartment and had him admitted to the jail."

"But that makes no sense!" Helen protested. "If David really had knocked Winthrop down, why should he take care to return him to his own coach and thereby incriminate himself?"

Uncle Josiah spread his hands wide. "Excellent question, my dear, and one I'll certainly bring up at David's hearing."

"What of—the other man?" Helen knew it was Nathaniel, but she couldn't be sure if her uncle did. If Nathaniel was at risk of being arrested, she'd have to warn him, little though he might wish to see her.

"David wouldn't name him so he could prevent him from also being imprisoned."

"He's willing to die to protect someone else?" Cassandra whispered.

Aunt Anne moved to the couch on Cassandra's other side and placed an arm around her niece. "There, there. It won't come to that, I'm sure."

Helen looked sharply at her uncle. "How strong is the case against David?"

"According to Governor Morley, there was a public altercation at High Street Market between David and Winthrop a few weeks ago in which David threatened Winthrop."

Helen blanched. "That's not what happened. Winthrop took offense to something David said and threatened to challenge David to a duel. David told Winthrop to name his second, and Winthrop backed down."

"Be that as it may, David has confessed to knocking down Winthrop at the docks."

"No!" Cassandra rasped.

Uncle Josiah hurried to clarify David's confession. "He says it wasn't a killing blow and that Winthrop was threatening him with a pistol. The constable found Winthrop's pistol at the dock where this all happened."

Cassandra gripped David's wrapper so tightly her knuckles went white. "Couldn't it belong to someone else?"

Uncle Josiah shook his head. "It's a dueling pistol engraved with Winthrop's monogram."

Aunt Anne shook her head. "There must be another explanation. Nobody who knows David would believe him capable of murdering Winthrop over a petty argument."

Helen wrinkled her nose. She wondered if she should say something. "I believe I know what they were arguing over," she began, but Uncle Josiah held up a hand to stop her.

"I've a suspicion I also know, but I'd rather not have it confirmed. I intend to represent David before the magistrate and would prefer not to have to prevaricate. David has said only that he went to meet someone, an act which is not illegal. No evidence whatsoever points to any significance to this meeting. If, for example, it was discovered that smuggling was going on, David would be at risk to lose all his property as well as his liberty."

"But he'd have his life!" Cassandra's voice was strained.

Uncle Josiah leaned across and patted his niece's hand. "Don't worry overmuch. There's not much evidence a murder took place—just an unfortunate accident. I plan to petition the magistrate to dismiss the charges."

Helen looked sideways at Cassandra, not wanting to upset her. "Winthrop mentioned that his father was very close to the magistrate."

"That is true," Uncle Josiah acknowledged.

Cassandra scoffed. "Surely, being the son of the Marquess of Dorset counts for something."

Uncle Josiah smiled wryly. "Yes, my dear, I suspect it will."

"Can David return home before the trial by paying a bond of some kind?" Helen asked. Cassandra looked up with a hopeful expression.

"Unfortunately, a bond is prohibited for those charged in a capital murder case. But never fear—I'll do all I can to see this is resolved quickly."

Cassandra turned her wedding ring around her finger. "Uncle—I believe you practice mostly in business and estate matters of the law. Are you sure—are you quite sure that you are familiar with this kind of case?" Her tone betrayed her embarrassment at having to ask such a question.

He smiled to show he hadn't taken offense. "When I first began practicing in the colonies, I took every case I could. It's only been in the last few years that I was able to focus on the more lucrative clients to be found in business and estate law."

Aunt Anne cut in. "Your uncle is very modest, my dears, but he made quite a name for himself defending criminal cases. He still receives letters from all over the New World asking for his legal advice!"

"I'm quite satisfied," Cassandra assured them. "I'm sorry that I asked. I feel as though my heart will burst from worry."

"There's no need to apologize," Aunt Anne assured her. "I would be out of my mind with worry if my husband were in a similar situation. You must try to settle your mind, however— for the baby."

Cassandra nodded tightly. "I'll try."

Aunt Anne turned to Helen. "Did you recall that there was to be a meeting of the society today?"

Helen gasped. "Oh! I quite forgot. I hate to leave Cassandra, though." Her sister seemed barely able to support herself.

"I could stay with her, but if you take my advice, you will postpone the meeting. Temperance has been made quite prostrate with grief over Winthrop's death, and I fear any confrontation would be harmful to both of you."

"Oh dear," Helen stammered, "I-I'm so sorry. I didn't even think about what she must be going through." Winthrop had seemed a worthless young man, but there was no denying Temperance's sincere affection for him.

"She'll be all right," Uncle Josiah assured her. "The attachment between them was not great. It only existed in Temperance's mind, I believe."

"It was no less real to her than if it had been a recognized engagement," Aunt Anne chided him gently. "In fact, I must return to her soon. Is there aught we can do for you?"

Helen looked at her sister. "No," she replied. "Thank you for coming."

"Uncle," Cassandra asked as they stood to leave, "when you say you will try to move quickly, what do you mean?

Could David return home today?"

"Unfortunately, the magistrate is out of town, but he will return early next week."

"Next week!" Cassandra gasped. "Oh, my poor husband! May I go to him?"

"The jail is no place for a woman of delicate sensibility," he insisted.

"If it is no place for me, then it is no place for him!"

Uncle Josiah shook his head. "They'd not let you enter."

"Remember to calm yourself," Aunt Anne urged Cassandra. "For your baby."

Cassandra's head hung. "Yes."

Cassandra continued to pace the drawing room despite her words, wringing her hands and growing distressed enough to cause Helen concern. Half an hour after the visitors departed, she convinced Cassandra to take some laudanum and rest once more.

Helen went to her own room to change into a woolen gown and petticoat and arranged her hair in a simple knot under a cap. After she finished dressing, she sat in the drawing room, head in hands. The situation was about as dire as she could imagine. David on trial for Winthrop's murder? It was unimaginable. Uncle Josiah simply had to succeed in getting the charges dismissed.

Helen looked up when another knock sounded at the door. Had Uncle Josiah come back again?

Westing admitted Jane Allen into the drawing room. "Oh, Jane. My apologies. You've found us quite . . ." Helen wasn't sure what to say and indicated for Jane to sit.

Jane made no mention of David's arrest, whether because the story hadn't traveled around, or Jane was as unobtrusively polite as ever, Helen couldn't know. "I came to tell you that Mr. Morris has returned to town, but perhaps it isn't a good time for you to go and speak to him?"

Helen hadn't given the indentured girl a moment's thought since the previous evening's events. "I'm afraid I can't leave my sister alone right now. Would you go to speak to Mr. Morris? I'll give you all the money we collected." She stood to fetch the purse from her room.

"I can't." Jane bit her lip in distress. "Mr. Morris is our landlord. If for some reason he grows upset by the offer, I can't risk him knowing I had anything to do with the business."

That seemed a concern Jane should've brought up earlier, but Helen didn't voice the observation. She looked to the doorway. Cassandra should be asleep for a few hours after the dose of laudanum, but if she awoke early and found Helen gone, she might be even more distressed.

Still, it was unlikely she'd wake, and it would be good to set at least one thing to rights. "I suppose I can go and try to make it back very quickly. Allow me to leave word with the servants."

Helen fetched the purse and informed Westing of her destination before setting off with Jane at a brisk clip. Jane pointed out the correct house when they reached Mulberry Street and then stood several houses down while Helen knocked.

A boy answered the door, far too young to be the harasser of any lady servants. "I am here to see Mr. Morris," Helen announced.

"He's not home. I suppose you'll be wanting my mother." Before Helen could stop him, he called out. "Ma! Lady to see you!"

He scurried off, leaving a confused Helen in the doorway. Jane had warned of the dangers of speaking to the lady of the house. Did Helen have time to get away before Mrs. Morris returned?

"Yes?" A middle-aged lady made her way down the stairs.

Apparently, Helen would have to try Mrs. Morris after all. "Good afternoon. I am Miss Helen Crofton. I realize this visit is unannounced, but I've a proposition to make to you."

Mrs. Morris scrutinized Helen while Helen did the same to her hostess, who dressed in the style of a much younger woman—many flounces and bows and a lace cap with a large red ribbon.

"Perhaps you know my uncle, Josiah Hayes?" Helen prompted after a few moments' uncomfortable silence. Despite his wealth and prominence in Philadelphia society, she dared not mention David's name in case the news really had spread, and it prompted the woman to question Helen about his arrest.

Mrs. Morris sniffed. "Follow me."

Helen followed her hostess into a small, overwrought drawing room stuffed with all manner of plates, badly painted landscapes, and embroidered cushions that could have passed as a shop selling tasteless decorations.

"Make yourself comfortable, Miss Crofton." Mrs. Morris pointed to a chair. "What brings you here?"

It was probably best to be honest about her intentions. "I believe you own a young lady's indenture."

Mrs. Morris inclined her head. "Yes, Mary. She's just upstairs, sewing. We've taken many such young girls out of Christian charity. They need a woman to watch over them. I shudder to think where some young girls end up when they make that perilous journey from England!"

Helen reminded herself she must be polite at all costs, though she badly wanted to tell Mrs. Morris she'd heard the goings-on here were far less than Christian in nature. She took a deep breath and began. "I'm a member of a charitable society. It's our mission—" She broke off, trying to consider how to word this delicately. "We'd like to offer opportunities to young girls to break their indentures and learn a useful trade. One of our members has put forward the name of your servant as a likely candidate. Of course, we would reimburse you for the remainder of her indenture."

Mrs. Morris shook her head sadly. "I'm afraid we have gotten too attached to Mary to give her up. She's become like another member of the family."

They weren't getting anywhere. Helen wondered if she should abandon the attempt and return another time when Mr. Morris was home. But what if Mrs. Morris wasn't as heartless as Jane feared, and her sympathy could be appealed to? "Mrs. Morris, I understand from a very trustworthy source that Mary isn't entirely happy here. Maybe you aren't aware that one of your sons has been harassing her?"

Mrs. Morris's eyes narrowed, and Helen's heart sank. She'd miscalculated again.

"That is a falsehood. I will call for her and let her tell you herself. Mary!" The woman went to the door and called in a loud voice.

A young girl quickly descended the stairs. She was very pretty, Helen noticed, but still looked more like a child than a woman.

"Mary, someone has been spreading rumors that you are unhappy here. Is this true?" Mrs. Morris demanded.

Mary stared at the floor. "No, ma'am."

"Do you know who started these rumors?"

"No, ma'am." Mary wouldn't look up.

"Has Mr. Jack bothered you?"

"No, ma'am," Mary whispered, barely audible.

Mrs. Morris raised an eyebrow at Helen. "Are you satisfied?"

Helen wasn't, but she didn't know what else she could do. She nodded tightly.

"Very well. Mary, be off. Now," Mrs. Morris said, turning back to Helen, "I don't know why you, a stranger, should be so impertinent as to come here and insult me based on unsubstantiated rumor!"

Helen took another deep breath. "I'm sorry. I must have misunderstood. Still, our society would very much like to proceed. We could compensate you as much as twenty pounds for the inconvenience of giving up your servant."

"Out of the question."

Helen's spirits fell. Had all their work been for naught?

"I couldn't think of letting her go for less than forty pounds," Mrs. Morris continued, "So that I might cover the wages of a hired girl until another servant can be found who satisfies our requirements."

Helen gaped at her audacity—to pretend she cared for Mary and then to ask for so much money. "A hired girl's wages can be no more than four pounds for an entire year!"

"I don't expect a young, unmarried lady such as yourself to understand household affairs." Mrs. Morris cocked her head and smirked. "Well, perhaps not so very young." She shook out her overly ruffled underskirt.

Helen ignored the barb. "There's no way our society can pay that much."

"That's a pity. Well, if you change your mind, you know where to return." Mrs. Morris stood and gestured towards the door. "Oh, and Miss Crofton? I should hate to hear any more of these rumors. My husband owns this row of buildings, did you know? If I found out that any of my neighbors were involved with spreading vicious rumors about my family, I would certainly have to ask him to evict the troublemakers. Good day."

Helen hurried away from the Morris's as quickly as she could manage, a sick feeling twisting in her stomach. Jane had disappeared, else Helen would have warned her about Mrs. Morris's threat. Helen would just have to write Jane a note explaining everything. She didn't want to risk leaving Cassandra too long.

Helen hadn't thought things could get any worse, but her bad judgment had now put Jane and her family at risk, not to mention poor Mary, who'd surely suffer on account of Helen's mismanagement.

Helen should've made up a lie when Mrs. Morris appeared rather than expose Jane to the very persecution she'd feared. She certainly shouldn't have tried to appeal to such a woman.

If David wasn't in prison, Helen would swallow her pride and ask him to pay the difference so she could free Mary at once, but she could hardly ask Cassandra for the use of fifteen pounds. Her sister didn't need anything further to trouble herself with, and if David was convicted of smuggling and lost everything, they'd need every penny they could get their hands on just to survive.

Not two days prior, David had been a free man, Helen had been proud of her work with the Society, and Nathaniel had been interested in courting her. She'd ruined the lives of nearly everyone she cared about in no time at all.

She simply couldn't return to the society and present her great failure, nor could she leave poor Mary to suffer for Helen's mistakes.

With a lurch in her stomach, she realized there was another way. An unpleasant way, but she wouldn't shirk. Even if the ladies in the society wished her to step down as president due to all her mistakes, she'd feel better if she could fix one.

Chapter 18

In the three days following the thwarted smuggling attempt, Nathaniel managed to talk to Misters Goodwin and Allen and work out a deal to pay Matlack half of the promised fee once the *Raleigh's* cargo was sold. Nathaniel hadn't planned to pay the balance if the plan went awry, but he couldn't risk the man spreading talking about what he'd seen in retaliation. Matlack hadn't wanted to wait, but he'd understood the need to stay silent or lose any chance of being paid.

The only thing remaining was to get David to reveal which magistrate had taken his case, as no one speaking of the matter in the taverns or on the streets seemed to have any idea. Early Monday morning, he presented himself at the jail, determined he'd make things right.

Two burly guards stood outside a wooden door and waved Nathaniel to go inside. "Jus' raise a noise when yer finished."

Nathaniel nodded curtly, hoping they wouldn't mistake him for an inmate of the facility when it was time to depart. Though if David could walk free in his stead, he'd gladly stay and allow the man to return to his wife.

The room was large, filled with at least a dozen men. A few sat in isolation, but the rest sat in a large group playing speculation with an odd assortment of buttons, pebbles, and other small trinkets in place of chips. The foul odor of the room reminded Nathaniel of being trapped below deck with sailors who hadn't bathed in weeks.

When David noticed Nathaniel, he threw down his cards. "Someone else can deal for a while." Groans and protests came from the men. "Now, now, I'll not be away forever."

Nathaniel tried not to stare at David, but his shock at seeing his friend in such disarray was too great. David had lost both his coat and his waistcoat's buttons, and he was severely in need of a shave. It was especially disconcerting to see David without a wig. He kept his hair more closely shorn than Nathaniel would have imagined.

"I'm sorry," Nathaniel finally managed to say.

"As am I. I can't believe Winthrop is dead." David shook his head sadly. "I'd no idea I struck him that hard. I feel wretched."

Nathaniel could scarcely believe it himself. "You were defending my life in a difficult situation. I'm the one who bears responsibility. If it wasn't for me, you'd not be here."

David waved a hand. "That's hardly true. It was foolish of me to quarrel with Winthrop in such a public space, although I never thought I was enacting a motive for murder."

"Winthrop was behaving insufferably towards Helen, and that fight wouldn't have signified anything if I hadn't asked you to help me at the docks," Nathaniel argued. "I should never have allowed you to be a part of the scheme."

David frowned. "I don't recall you entreating me to

involve myself. If I remember correctly, I offered to help."

That was true enough, but Nathaniel ought to have refused. "You have a family. I should have found someone else."

"I imagine I'll still have a family when I emerge from this pit." David closed his eyes for a moment as if in pain. "How does Cassandra fare? I've gotten reports from Josiah Hayes, but I'm sure you've seen more of her in your visits with Helen."

Nathaniel shoved his hands into the pockets of his black wool coat. "I last saw Helen on Saturday, and your wife not at all."

David raised an eyebrow. "You have a fascinating method of courting my sister-in-law."

"The last time I visited Helen without your permission, you were none too pleased."

He should just tell David the truth, but for some reason, he was hesitant to explain what had happened.

"I was young and in love once. I hardly think I could have scared myself off. You cannot expect to win fair lady by acting so indecisively."

"You're still both young and in love," Nathaniel couldn't resist pointing out.

"Yes, I am." David's shoulders slumped. "Which is why I'm asking you to personally visit my wife and sister at this time and ensure they are well."

There was nothing for it. Nathaniel had to tell him. "I can't."

David stared at Nathaniel for a moment, and then his eyes narrowed. "You're not trifling with Helen, are you?"

"Of course not," Nathaniel replied, louder than he intended, and some of the card players looked over at them. He lowered his voice. "All my money was sunk to the bottom of the Delaware River Saturday night. I'd never insult Helen by courting her when I have nothing to offer but debt and poverty."

"Have you spoken to Helen about this?" David demanded.

"I have."

David raised an eyebrow in disbelief.

"She doesn't wish to see me again, which is why I can't go back to your home."

"Are you certain that's what she wants? What precisely did you say to each other?"

"That's not important," Nathaniel insisted.

David shook his head. "You probably said something to upset her. You must go to her at once and beg her forgiveness."

The conversation had grown entirely ridiculous. Nathaniel was there to help David, not discuss the affairs of his heart. "That's the least of our worries right now." David opened his mouth as if to argue, but Nathaniel pushed ahead. "Which magistrate has taken your case?"

David blinked. "Hickson. Why?"

"No matter. Well, I can see that you're holding up. Good day." Nathaniel turned to go.

David grabbed his arm. "Nathaniel, come back here. You're not thinking of doing anything stupid like confess to a crime you didn't commit, are you?"

"Wouldn't you rather me take your place so you can return to your wife?" Nathaniel lowered his voice to the merest whisper. "I'll say I'm the one who struck Winthrop, and you can go home."

"You must be joking!" David scoffed. "I've kept your name out on purpose—no sense in you getting thrown in here next to me. Besides, you're a little late. Westing already tried to take my place. He brought a bottle of my finest spirits to try to bribe the guard. I soon sent him packing and gave him a round scolding for trying to dispose of my goods that way."

"Your wife is with child. Surely you don't wish to leave her a widow?" Nathaniel knew what it was to grow up without a father, and he'd not wish it on any child.

"Of course not!" David put a hand on Nathaniel's shoulder. "But it won't come to that. I know Morley is furious, but I fully depend on the magistrate to let me go free. He's one of those toad-eaters who is always on the lookout for ways to ingratiate himself with great men." He wrinkled his nose in disgust, and Nathaniel marveled that David could manage to look so disreputable and aristocratic at the same time.

"But if that doesn't work—"

"Right now, all Morley has is a few witnesses from the market saying Winthrop and I quarreled and the testimony of his coachman that I deposited Winthrop alive into Morley's own coach. Josiah assures me that's very thin evidence to build a murder case. Bringing your name into things could add smuggling and money to the discussion—far more convincing motives for murder. I need you to stay out of this."

David's commanding tone left no room for argument. Nathaniel put both hands in the air. "Very well; I'll abide by what you have to say. Do you need anything?" He couldn't just leave David and go on with his life—not that he had much business to attend to.

"Other than my wife in my arms? A hot bath, clean linens, and a shave." David shrugged. "I fear they'll have to wait a little longer. Josiah tells me Hickson has been visiting friends outside of town ever since he was assigned to my trial."

"Ho there, your lordship!" one of the men called. "We aren't gettin' any younger!"

"Ah, my retinue." David squeezed Nathaniel's shoulder, dismissing him. "Thank you for coming. I hope to see you next under more favorable circumstances."

Nathaniel was able to leave as easily as he entered, though he fancied he was the recipient of many suspicious glares. The jail was enormous, built to replace the overcrowded facility on High Street. It seemed the more the city grew, the more the crime did as well.

He shivered a little in the chilly air and knew they'd soon see more snow. A seaman could always judge the weather.

He wished it were as easy for him to judge what he should do. David's points were valid, but what if he was wrong and the magistrate wasn't swayed by David's family name? If David was found guilty, Nathaniel's admitting to the crime was unlikely to do anything. Perhaps Nathaniel should get Josiah Hayes's opinion.

Hopefully, he could speak to the man without accidentally presenting himself to Helen. He couldn't imagine either one of them wished for a painful reminder of what they'd lost.

He frowned to himself, thinking of David's disbelief that the relationship had ended. But how could David be expected to understand Nathaniel's predicament when he had plenty of money to keep his family in comfort? When David had asked for Cassandra's hand, likely the only question was how soon they would marry.

As Nathaniel approached Hayes's law office, he discovered men, women, and children packing the streets around the Pennsylvania State House. Nathaniel tried to think of why anyone would gather, but he'd not had much other than tea on his mind the last few weeks. Perhaps he'd missed something important.

As he edged through the crowd, he picked up phrases from conversations around him.

"'Tis a mockery of honest men!"

"We'll not stand for it this time."

"Boston will not fail us! She and New York will stand with us!"

The *Polly* must have finally docked with the East India Company tea, he realized. Someone handed him a broadside issued by "The Committee for Tarring and Feathering," warning that the captain of the *Polly* should expect swift retribution if he tried to unload his cargo in the city.

Nathaniel shouldered his way almost to the steps of the State House.

"Carter!" someone yelled.

Nathaniel turned around to see Humphrey Goodwin.

"How goes it? Come to see Captain Ayres off?"

"What's going on in there?" Nathaniel pointed at the State House.

"They're voting on resolutions as to how to respond. The *Polly* just docked this morning, but they say Captain Ayres is too afraid to step onto dry land. Ah, have you met Phineas Brand and Sebastian Linch? They're in your line of work."

Brand was tall and wiry, with red hair tied into a queue, while Linch was short and stocky and wore an inexpensive gray wig. "We've met." Nathaniel bowed to the merchants.

"'Tis about time we run those tyrants out of the city," Brand said. "I've paid a king's ransom to hold my cargo in a warehouse in Chester."

Linch nodded. "Aye, I sent mine to Virginia and had to sell

it at a loss."

They all looked to Nathaniel. "I had to dump mine," he admitted.

Goodwin screwed up his face as if he'd just bitten a lemon but otherwise said nothing about the financial loss he shared in, apparently having taken Nathaniel's warnings not to admit his involvement to heart.

Brand shook his head. "Some of us have talked of starting a private insurance scheme amongst ourselves. We would each pay a small amount and could make claims against a general fund the next time King George decides to try and put us out of business."

"Lloyd's of London is the place to go for insurance," Goodwin interjected, sounding as proud of the establishment as if it were his own.

Nathaniel blinked at the man's idiocy. "Lloyd's doesn't insure smuggled goods."

Linch cut his eyes towards Goodwin, then turned to Nathaniel. "We're meeting to talk of this at City Tavern later if you want to join us."

Nathaniel had a refusal on the tip of his tongue. He didn't trust other people to make decisions that could affect his business. Still, if he'd been able to insure the cargo, he wouldn't have worried about smuggling it, and David wouldn't be in prison.

"I thank you for the offer," he finally replied. "I don't have the coin to invest in cargo at the moment, much less insurance, but if that changes, I should be pleased to join you." Brand and Linch inclined their heads towards him.

The doors to the state house opened, and a group of men hurried out.

"We've passed the resolutions!" Dr. Benjamin Rush declared.

A cry of approval rose up. "Follow me to the docks, and we'll send the *Polly* on her way!"

Slowly the enormous crowd trickled towards the docks. Nathaniel tried in vain to work his way to the edge of the crowd, but his attempt was futile, and he found himself swept along with it instead.

A man perched in a tree counted people as they passed. He met Nathaniel's eyes and gestured towards himself. "This may be the largest group of people ever assembled in the colonies," he explained. "We are witnessing history. I intend to write about it in my newspaper."

Nathaniel only bowed and let the crowd carry him on, unsure the man was correct. Why would history care about such an event? He'd be happy if he could find a way to repay his creditors, with a little left over to send his empty ships for new goods.

That wasn't strictly true, he realized. He'd be less anxious about the future if he could manage that, but he wouldn't be happy. If he was honest with himself, the only thing that would bring him real joy was a life with Helen.

Such thoughts brought a curious ache in his chest, but rubbing at the spot did nothing.

Helen couldn't feel the loss as keenly. She hadn't tried to dissuade him when he'd explained his financial situation or said she would wait for him to regain his livelihood. Not that he'd ask that of her. It might be years before he again had the means to support a wife, if ever. She was beautiful and clever, and she'd find another man to marry. One who could give her the life she deserved.

By the time Nathaniel arrived at the dock, Captain Ayres had already been confronted and agreed to leave. Another cheer sprang up among the crowd, and some people started singing a hymn. A little child in front of him waved a flag that had Benjamin Franklin's old "Join-or-Die" cartoon painted on it. Perhaps history *would* remember the day, judging by the number of people who found the event meaningful.

Eventually, Nathaniel nudged his way out of the crowd and started to take a circuitous route to the law office.

What was he doing? David had asked him to stay out of the business. But could Nathaniel just sit by and trust that David had everything in hand?

Nathaniel's judgment hadn't served anyone very well. Perhaps all he could do was await good tidings.

With a sigh, he turned for his warehouse. He'd never been able to just sit around waiting for anything. He hardly thought there was anything he could do to improve his financial difficulties, but there had to be something he could try.

Chapter 19

Helen faced quite a different assembly than the one she'd presided over at the Society's previous meeting. David was passing his third day in jail, and Cassandra had elected to stay home in case he returned. Temperance still refused to leave her room, and the usually calm Jane sat with a troubled expression.

Though she wished she could mend things with Temperance and Jane, Helen was relieved Cassandra hadn't accompanied her. She'd had an errand to complete before the meeting, and she wasn't sure if Cassandra would support it.

Euphemia was the only one at the meeting in high spirits, unable to stop speaking of the events at the State House. "My father was there, did I mention? I begged him and begged him, but I could not prevail upon him to take me, though I found out later that my own maid attended, for she was out at the market that day to purchase a new pair of stockings for me."

Helen let Euphemia continue uninterrupted, hoping to prevent the inevitable moment where the society discovered her failures.

"Is that a new cap?" Constance asked, passing Helen a cup of tea during a lull in Euphemia's commentary. "I don't think I've ever seen you wear that one before."

Helen reached a hand up and patted the cap absent-mindedly. "Oh—yes."

Finally, even Euphemia ran out of things to say. Helen stood reluctantly. "I call this meeting to order." She looked at the secretary and found Patience already had a quill poised to record the minutes. "I've something to report regarding our mission."

Euphemia clapped in delight, but Helen couldn't manage to turn her grimace into a smile. "I made a grave error." It was best to be honest and not try to conceal the extent of her failures. "I confronted the woman who holds the indenture we meant to purchase, despite receiving advice not to. She insists we pay her forty pounds. She's also threatened the home of one of our members." Though Helen didn't name Jane, all eyes turned to look at her. Helen winced. She hadn't meant to spread Jane's business about. She tried to regain their attention. "I plan to resign as president of this society."

"But—" Patience began.

Helen held up a hand. "Please, let me finish, and then I'll sit down or leave or whatever you all think best. At this time, we have thirty-four pounds. I'll do anything you think best to find the remainder of the funds. In fact—" She reached up and pulled off her cap. All eyes were affixed to the sight of Helen's shorn head. "I've already sold my hair to a wigmaker. He said it was particularly fine and offered me eight pounds for it." Her voice trembled a little at the last.

Euphemia gasped. "Oh, Helen! How brave you are! You

quite inspire me."

"You're very good." Constance sounded overawed.

Helen shook her head. "I'm neither brave nor good. I only did what I could to resolve the misfortunes I've brought upon the society."

Patience sighed heavily. "I wish you'd spoken to me before you took such a drastic step. I could've informed you it's forbidden to sell the indenture of a young person at a price over twenty-five pounds."

"What?" Helen stared at her younger cousin in disbelief.

"It's the law. To prevent exploitation."

Euphemia gasped. "You didn't have to sell your hair after all!"

Helen only shook her head. The society might not need the money her hair supplied, but she'd needed to feel she was contributing something to make up for her mistakes.

"Papa will go and talk to that woman," Constance announced. Helen recalled how her sweet cousin had managed to get Uncle Josiah to buy out all their tarts. Constance might be just the person to succeed her as president.

Jane spoke up hesitantly. "She doesn't have to sell the contract." Jane was right, and her suggestion of making gingerbread over tarts would undoubtedly have made life easier during their market days. Perhaps she'd make a good president.

Patience looked up from the minutes she'd continued to record. "She'll sell the contract. She could be sued if the girl can prove she was mistreated." Helen smiled weakly at Patience, who was dedicated and intelligent enough to make an excellent president.

Euphemia stood up. "May I speak?" Helen motioned for her friend to stand. Euphemia was so kind and good at putting people at ease that she'd probably make a very good president as well. Especially if she could get her father to contribute to every cause he grew weary with. "Helen, I cannot bear for you to step down as president."

"I think it's best—" Helen began.

Euphemia interrupted Helen to assert herself. "No, it's my turn to speak, I believe?" Patience nodded. "And I say that you've been a wonderful president, no matter what you think. Nobody could have worked harder than you did at planning everything and standing outside in the cold day after day."

Helen had to bite her tongue from repeating just how badly she'd ruined things with Mrs. Morris. Rules were rules, and Euphemia had the floor.

"Let's put it to a vote," Patience suggested. "All in favor of retaining Helen in the office of president?" Everyone raised a hand, even Jane. "The 'ayes' have it!"

Helen could hardly believe they wished to give her a second chance, but perhaps they didn't account her failures as significantly as she did.

She received permission to speak again and got to her feet. "I thank you for your trust in me, even if I don't feel it's deserved." She swallowed hard, willing herself not to grow tearful. "We have a little more money than we need to pay off Mary's contract. Are there any ideas for what we should do?"

"Why don't we continue our operation?" Patience suggested. "We could purchase the contracts of young women at the indenture market as they arrive in Philadelphia and find them paid employment instead."

"That's a wonderful idea." Helen called for a vote, and the motion passed.

As the ladies gathered their cloaks to return home, Helen

slipped over to speak to Patience. "How is Temperance?"

Patience offered Helen a sad smile. "Still quite distraught. News of Winthrop's death came as quite an unpleasant shock."

"Would it help if I went up to speak to her?" Helen motioned towards the stairs leading to the girls' shared bedroom.

"Probably best if you don't." Patience didn't have to explain further. Helen's dislike of Winthrop hadn't been a secret, and she wouldn't wish to cause Temperance any pain.

Helen spoke to Jane next. "Would you like me to ask my uncle to intercede with Mrs. Morris about your home as well?"

"Thank you, but we're behind with the rent as it is. I think it's time for us to move on." Jane lowered her eyes in embarrassment.

Helen hadn't meant to make her feel worse. "Please let me know if there's anything I can do for you."

Jane agreed.

Helen made her way towards the door, unsure what to make of the meeting's outcome. Was she to consider herself as having succeeded as president because Mary would soon be free? She could hardly celebrate with Jane and Temperance so troubled and David still in prison.

Euphemia grabbed onto Helen's arm on the street in front of the house. "May I walk with you for a few moments? I had something particular I wished to tell you."

"Of course." Helen suggested that it made more sense for her to escort Euphemia to her home since it was so near. "What was it you wished to say?"

Euphemia beamed at her. "Just how delighted I am that you're my friend. I've admired you for ever so long, but I worried I was too silly for you to like me."

Helen blushed a little. She'd once thought Euphemia a bit daft, but over the last few weeks she'd grown to appreciate Euphemia's good nature. She was honest in her reply. "I'm very proud to know you."

"And I you," Euphemia returned. They parted as friends at the Goodwins' doorstep.

Helen walked towards her home with her heart a little lighter than it had been. Euphemia had wished to be her friend even before Helen had proven anything about her leadership ability, and the society wished her to stay on as president despite all the mistakes she'd made. Surely that meant something, even if Helen had made other mistakes.

If only David would return and set Cassandra's heart at ease, Helen could be perfectly content. Her own little heartache was nothing compared to her sister's. Nathaniel hadn't done more than merely intend to court her.

And kissed her. And made her feel she was valuable just as she was.

But perhaps more than just Euphemia had thought that all along.

Helen pulled her cloak tighter around herself, though it made little difference in the cold November air. It was even possible Nathaniel could find it in his heart to forgive her, though that seemed very unlikely if she couldn't find a way to return his money to him. Helen wasn't sure how much a cargo hold full of tea was worth, but she was sure it would take more than selling her hair to the wigmaker to recoup Nathaniel's losses.

She might think of something if she set her mind to it.

Chapter 20

Cassandra paced in the drawing room when Helen arrived home, still wearing David's wrapper, but at least Helen had coaxed her to bathe and change her shift the day before.

"Is there any news?" Cassandra demanded.

Helen squeezed Cassandra's hands. "I didn't find Uncle at his home or the law office. Perhaps he's with David."

"It's maddening not to know anything! I must see David for myself." Cassandra turned toward the doorway.

"Wait!" Helen laid a hand on her sister's arm. "They don't even allow women in the jail, Uncle Josiah told us."

"They'll not be able to stop me. Uncle's reports are not enough—I know he would lie to me if he thought it was for my own good."

"Westing reported David is in good spirits," Helen countered.

Her sister scoffed. "Westing would certainly lie to me on David's order."

Helen couldn't argue with that. "Let me go and ask the clerks if they know where Uncle Josiah is."

Cassandra turned to face Helen. "Has Nathaniel been to see David? I think I could trust him not to embellish the truth."

Helen bit her lip. She still hadn't mentioned what happened to Cassandra. "I haven't seen Nathaniel since Saturday."

"But all the times you've gone out—"

"I've only left on society business."

"And Nathaniel hasn't come to see you." It wasn't a question. Cassandra focused all her attention on Helen in a way she hadn't since David's imprisonment.

Helen swallowed. "He blames me for alerting Governor Morley to David's absence at the ball. I cost Nathaniel a great sum—perhaps even his whole livelihood."

"That's ridiculous." Cassandra sat upon the couch and cradled her rounded belly. "The plan always sounded very risky to me. Too risky, and I told David that. He assured me time and again they'd be in no danger and that he'd be perfectly safe." Her voice dripped with frustration.

"It sounds as if they might have managed it if I hadn't taken it upon myself to distract the governor." Helen shuddered at the memory of that awful night.

Cassandra patted the spot next to her, and Helen sat. "Perhaps, but they might have just as easily been found out the next morning when Nathaniel tried to move the tea to market. It's unbelievable he'd put all the blame on you!"

It made perfect sense to Helen. "It sounds as if he's had a very difficult life. He's very protective of all he's accomplished."

Cassandra's eyes narrowed. "And that gives him leave to blame you when his smuggling attempt goes wrong?"

"No, I only mean that it's understandable for him to be

upset with the person that lost him the things he's been working towards for years."

"Then he should be angry with himself." Cassandra folded her arms. "It didn't have to be smuggling. David told me. Nathaniel could've sold the tea at a loss, repaid his creditors, and sent his ship out again."

"I don't pretend to understand business matters." Helen spread her hands out wide.

Cassandra's crack of laughter startled her. "Yes, your success with the tart sales was purely accidental. You didn't work night and day to see it a success."

"I did work very hard, but in the end, we earned most of the money from donations." Donations Helen hadn't even wanted to take. Had her opposition to accepting David's money been foolish all along?

"I'm sorry. I know how much you wanted to prove that ladies could do such a thing without assistance."

Helen sighed. "It would have been ridiculous to refuse funds that could free Mary even faster."

Cassandra looked up. "Is she free, then?"

"She will be soon." Helen recited the visit to Mrs. Morris and the subsequent society meeting, though she left one part out. "And Euphemia said after the meeting she'd always wished to be my friend."

Cassandra smiled at Euphemia's kindness. "I told you they liked you, even when you thought they did not. Perhaps you're wrong about Nathaniel, and he isn't angry at all."

Helen shook her head. "His words were very clear."

"He said, 'Helen, I am furious with you, and I never wish to see you again?'" Cassandra pressed.

"Not exactly." Helen struggled to recall his remarks. She

could more easily remember the feelings of guilt and anguish than his precise words.

"Even if he was angry when you first told him what happened, a man in love will overlook much greater faults."

"In love?" Helen repeated. "He never spoke to me of love. He only wished to court me."

Cassandra laughed again. "Where do you think courtship leads, dearest?"

Helen rested her head against her sister's shoulder. "I only want a husband who will love me as much as David loves you."

Cassandra let out a long sigh. "I can hardly wait for David to return."

"So you can tell him you were right about the smuggling plot being dangerous?" Helen asked.

"No! First, I'll kiss him, and then I'll lecture him."

Helen laughed. "An excellent plan. If I ever do manage to find a husband, I'll know precisely how to go on."

"If you want it to be Nathaniel, I daresay he'll need a little encouragement."

"I wish I could get his money back for him." Helen sighed deeply. "I can't imagine how."

"You could do as Euphemia suggested and sell your hair," Cassandra teased.

Helen stiffened.

"Helen? You didn't!"

Helen sat up and pulled the cap from her head. "I wanted to present as much money as I could when I told the society how badly the meeting with Mrs. Morris went."

Cassandra reached out a hand and gingerly patted the twisted pieces pinned on top of Helen's head. "It's not bad. I couldn't even tell when you had your cap on."

"But I'll not be able to dress my hair for any formal occasions." The loss was a little more painful than Helen liked to admit.

"You could get a wig." Cassandra started to laugh. "Perhaps of your own hair!"

Helen joined in laughing with her sister at the ridiculous notion until tears rolled down both of their cheeks. "Do you think David would lend me the money to buy back my hair?"

Cassandra wiped her eyes with the back of her hands. "He'll probably insist upon it."

Knowing David, Helen could well believe it. "I'm not sure how many lifetimes of hair sales it would take until I paid Nathaniel back."

"Has he ever said anything to you to indicate he'd expect you to do that, much less accept money from you?"

Helen thought about Nathaniel's offering to pay for the broken vase just because David had asked him to escort her home. "No."

Cassandra nodded astutely. "I would be very surprised indeed if he thought anything of the sort. There's been some misunderstanding between the two of you. You must find a way to speak to him."

Hope rose in Helen at her sister's words. "But what if he is still angry, and he thinks me a foolish, irritating woman who's come to pester him when he wants nothing to do with me?"

Cassandra's eyebrows lifted. "I shouldn't think you'd want to marry a man who felt that way about you. I do think you should consider a man who would take you just as you are and care for you all the days of your life."

Helen looked at her hands. Go to Nathaniel with no

solution to the problem she'd created for him and share her feelings for him? What would he think of her?

Cassandra smiled and patted Helen's hand as if she could discern her thoughts. Perhaps she could. "Come, I must dress in case David comes home. I must look my best to greet him."

Helen didn't wish to upset Cassandra, but she'd hate for her sister to get her hopes up for nothing. "We don't know if he'll come today." He could, but he could just as likely remain in jail many more days while the magistrate sorted everything out.

"Then I'll get dressed every day." Cassandra got to her feet and made her way to the doorway. She walked with confidence for the first time in days, as if she was moving right into her beloved's arms.

Helen trembled to think of what Nathaniel might think or say if she told him how she felt and asked him to accept her, but what if she could have a love of her very own?

She followed her sister out of the drawing room. "Come, let's make you ready."

Nathaniel made it back to his office and poured over his maps, trying to determine the smallest amount of money he'd need to borrow in order to make the largest return. Using rough calculations, he wrote out multiple scenarios that could work. He only needed the latest commodity prices to complete his plans.

And a loan, of course. The idea of borrowing more money when he already owed so much made him feel ill, but it was worth a chance rather than letting ships sit idle or selling them off to repay his debt. That was a loss he'd not soon recover from.

If he was careful and lucky, he might pay his investors and earn back all he'd lost in two or three years. Then, if he was truly fortunate and Helen remained unmarried, he'd address her once more.

Of course, that was as far-fetched as expecting to see a mermaid. A tale a man told himself, and nothing real. But it was all he had.

He walked out to try to speak to a banker he'd done business with in the past. Nathaniel would be honest about the source of his losses and share his plans. From what Brand and Linch said, he wasn't the only merchant who'd suffered under the governor's heightened restrictions. With any luck, the banker wouldn't turn Nathaniel away for being overextended.

Thankfully the crowds had dispersed as he walked toward the center of town for the second time that day. He probably had the cold air to thank for that. Nobody would linger overlong with such a chill wind blowing.

He passed the Walnut Street Jail with a heavy heart. Perhaps he'd return to visit David the next day and reassure him Nathaniel was doing all he could to repay David's investment. Perhaps he could take Cassandra word of her husband, though he was sure others were informing her of David's wellbeing.

As he approached the courthouse on Market Street, two figures emerged from the arched doorway—Josiah Hayes and David. Nathaniel picked up his steps.

"Nathaniel! Be the first to congratulate me on being a free man." David had found a coat from somewhere, a plain brown garment not up to his usual standard. Combined with his waistcoat's missing buttons, his lack of a wig, and his three days' beard, David resembled sailors Nathaniel knew.

Nathaniel clapped David on the back. "You did it!"

"Josiah did it, actually." David inclined his head towards his companion.

"I rather think David's name did it," Hayes retorted. "Well, unless you need me, I must away home. I promised Anne to return in time for supper."

David shook Hayes's hand vigorously. "Thank you for everything."

Josiah smiled. "My niece has been very anxious about you. Her happiness is my greatest reward."

"And I must reunite with her at once. Come, Nathaniel. I wish to speak to you about something. Walk me home unless you're otherwise engaged?" He glanced at the satchel on Nathaniel's shoulder.

"It can wait." Nathaniel bowed to Hayes and tried to match David's brisk pace. "Did they dismiss all the charges?"

"Every one. Seems Hickson wishes to return to England and didn't wish to risk angering my family. The joke is on him. They probably would have been delighted to hear I'd hanged."

Nathaniel winced. He hadn't exactly had a warm upbringing, but none of his relations would rejoice in his death.

David rubbed his hands together. "Now, we've a matter of business—"

"Yes, I was just going to see a banker about a loan. If approved, I have a plan to repay you."

"That's not at all what concerns me but do go on." David spoke as if he was indulging Nathaniel in letting him explain about the future of David's own money.

"The *Good King George* can take a load of corn to Jamaica and return with molasses. When the *Fair Albion* is ready to sail again, I'll either send another load of corn to the West Indies or perhaps pipe staves to Lisbon in exchange for port wine."

David wrinkled his nose. "Nobody in Philadelphia drinks port."

Nathaniel shrugged. "It will sell, albeit for less than Madeira." It was the best he could do with a small amount of capital to spend on the initial cargo.

"How much do you need?"

"I could do something with two hundred pounds." If he could borrow more, he'd fill his hold with the wheat they were so desperate for across the islands and return with rum.

"I'll give you five hundred."

Nathaniel made a derisive noise. "I already owe you that much." More, if he counted the return David was to have made on the tea.

"And loaning you money is my best chance to see the debt repaid," David countered.

Nathaniel couldn't let his friend make a poor investment, even if he did need the capital. "You'd just be throwing money away."

"This is the first time you've ever lost me a penny."

Nathaniel started to argue again, but David forestalled him.

"Is my money not good enough for you?" David sounded so genuinely hurt that Nathaniel began to feel as if he was a cur for refusing.

"Of course it is. I—I thank you." It was a kind gesture—not just the money, but the confidence.

"Excellent." David smiled broadly. "Now to the real business. We're almost to my home, so I don't have time to hear all you said to Helen. I only want your word that you'll talk to her and sort out all your problems."

"My business won't be solvent for another two years." Perhaps one, with David's large investment. Already Nathaniel did sums in his head. If he could get it, wheat would allow him to get a more expensive product in return—or perhaps even cash.

Josiah Hayes's law office was in sight, and David stepped even more quickly. "You're always taking risks and investing all your money on new cargos. It's the nature of your work."

"Would you court a woman knowing you couldn't keep her in comfort?"

David eyed him for a moment. "No," he finally admitted.

Nathaniel's heart sank. Even though he knew better, some part of him had wished for David to come up with a solution he hadn't thought of. "There you have it."

"But I still want you to talk to Helen about it. She might feel differently."

"I can't—it doesn't matter—" Nathaniel spluttered.

David came to a stop before his front door. "I'm not asking you as your investor. I'm asking as your friend. Will you speak to Helen?"

Nathaniel could hardly refuse. "I'm not sure she wants to see me."

"Wait here and I'll check." David clapped Nathaniel on the shoulder and let himself in the building.

Nathaniel shuffled in the cold and tried not to look up into David's drawing room window. How long should he wait before accepting she wasn't coming?

And what was he to say to her? Tell her he cared for her, and perhaps they could marry in a few years? It sounded like something a lad of fifteen might tell his sweetheart.

Still, if there was any chance he'd one day have his own home to return to, a home he made with Helen, he had to take it.

Besides, he could hardly make himself seem more ridiculous to her eyes.

With a sigh, he began to pace in front of the house to keep his feet from going numb while he waited.

Chapter 21

Helen was just pinning Cassandra's last curl in place when the sound of the door opening made them both jump.

"David?" Cassandra flew to the door, with Helen following close behind her. David was indeed standing in the front entry-way, arms wrapped around Cassandra, who neither kissed nor scolded him.

"I thought I lost you!" she cried.

"Never," David assured her. He brought one hand gently to the back of Cassandra's head and rubbed slow circles on her back with his other.

Love really did overlook a multitude of sins, Helen realized. David hadn't looked as terrible after he recovered from a mild case of smallpox a few years before, and he could certainly stand to take a long bath.

Wrinkling her nose, she started to move towards her room and give the couple privacy. "Glad to see you back," she called. They didn't appear to notice her.

Helen sat on her bed and wondered how to contrive a meeting with Nathaniel. Perhaps he would stop by to welcome David home. She could try to seek him out, though it really didn't do for a lady to visit a man in his home. She had only done so before in a dire emergency.

Did her desperate need to speak to him also count as an emergency? She grabbed her cloak and walked towards the door.

David and Cassandra were sitting next to each other on the couch. Helen was careful not to enter the room all the way to avoid the smell.

Cassandra looked truly happy for the first time in days. "Are you going out?"

"There's something I must do."

David smiled at her. "Yes, go outside and put poor Nathaniel out of his misery."

Helen's heart was seized by a sudden twist. "Nathaniel is here?"

"You left him out in the cold?" Cassandra sounded aghast.

"He wasn't sure Helen would want to see him."

"I, not wish to see him?" Helen repeated. "He's the one who doesn't wish to see me." Only, she wasn't sure anymore that was the meaning he'd intended when he told her he'd lost everything. What if he thought he was being noble by refusing to court her any longer?

David sighed and placed his head in his hands. "I knew it had to be something like this. Go down and talk to him."

Helen's feet didn't seem to want to move forward. David made it sound so easy.

Perhaps it was. "Very well."

"Helen," David called out. "Whatever happens, I want you

to know that you'll always have a home here."

"Yes," Cassandra agreed. "I should like to have you live as near to me as possible, including right here if that is what you wish."

David's eyes twinkled. "It will save us hundreds of pounds on hiring a nursemaid over the years."

His teasing settled Helen's racing heart. She smiled sweetly at her sister and brother-in-law "Thank you for reminding me of my worth." She made her way downstairs and out into the cold and found Nathaniel pacing in front of the law office.

"Good afternoon." Helen noted the setting sun. "Evening, rather." She pulled her cloak tight, teeth already chattering in the cold air.

"Good evening." Nathaniel's eyes rose to the drawing room window above their heads. "Is David inside?"

Had he not seen him go? "Yes, with my sister."

Nathaniel nodded. Perhaps David had been wrong, and he hadn't wished to speak to Helen at all.

She'd spent far too long mistaking Nathaniel. It was time they reached an understanding. "I'm glad you've come," she declared boldly. "I've wanted to speak to you."

"Have you?" Nathaniel's whole body relaxed as if she'd relieved him on a point of great anxiety.

The door to the law office opened behind Helen, and all of Uncle Josiah's clerks came filing out, Owen at the rear. Owen took one look at Helen and Nathaniel and scurried away from the door. "I won't lock up, as you're standing here."

Helen nodded, too distracted by her thoughts to pay the young man any more mind. She looked directly at Nathaniel. "I want you to know that I'm very sorry that I cost you your business. If I could think of any way to get your money back, I would. Hurting you was the very last thing I wished to do."

Nathaniel drew back. "What happened at the docks wasn't your fault."

"I led the governor right to you."

"I'm the one who chose to try smuggling." He took a step towards her. "I don't hold you responsible. Not at all."

"Then why did you wish not to see me again?" Helen had to be sure.

"Because that's what you wanted." He spoke as if the answer was obvious.

Helen let out a short laugh. It seemed David and Cassandra were right. It had all been a misunderstanding. She stepped towards the man she'd learned to respect. Whose company she'd grown to enjoy.

Cassandra said he'd require encouragement. "That's not at all what I wanted."

Helen stood within reach, smiling at him in a way that made him want to kiss her again, even in full view of the street. Some part of his mind was trying to remind him of something. Something important. A reason that this was a terrible idea.

He took a step back. "I can't court you for at least a year." He tried not to cringe at his awkward words.

"Why not?"

"I need to regain all the money I lost before I could afford to marry."

Helen's lips quirked. "Marry? You've only asked me to court you."

"I meant to court you until we married," Nathaniel admitted. Had she not shared that expectation?

She took cautious steps forward to once more close the gap between them. "What kind of things do you fancy you require in order to marry?"

"A house, for one." Money for the mantua maker, so Helen need not be ashamed by made-over garments. A coach, since she was used to one in David's household.

"You have lodgings," she pointed out. "I've been to them."

"They're well enough for a man alone, but you wouldn't be happy there."

"Wouldn't I?" She laid a hand on his arm. "The room was snug, but it's not impossible to imagine two people sharing it."

A family of five had occupied the space before Nathaniel. However, Helen deserved more. "I don't think you understand what I'm saying. Until I pay back the investors, we'd have to live simply. There would be no new gowns. No coach."

She moved her hand up until it was over his heart. "I still wish you to court me first before arranging all the details of our married lives, but I don't mind telling you I wouldn't miss those things if I was sharing a life with someone I love."

Did she mean that she loved him? Nathaniel reached for her, determined to kiss her right there, no matter that they were on the street. He felt her whole body trembling in his arms from the cold. "We must get you inside."

Helen led him through the law office door but made no move to go up the stairs. "Did you notice anything different about me?"

Nathaniel stared at Helen, but the law office's fires had

been banked, leaving the place too dark to make out much about her appearance. "Are you wearing a new gown?" That wasn't it; she was wearing a red gown he'd seen before.

"Not my gown." Helen sighed and pulled off the white cap atop her head. "All my hair was sold to a wigmaker. David will probably insist on rebuying it for me so I don't embarrass him."

Nathaniel reached out a hand and touched the hair, pinned in twists so it would stay up under her cap. "You'll probably start a new fashion."

"Says a man with only two coats." Her voice was warm and teasing.

He reached for her again, positioning his hands on her waist. "I know only one thing with certainty."

"And that is?"

"I can't imagine going on in life without your intelligence, your humor, your plans and hard work."

He heard Helen's short intake of breath. "Nathaniel."

He brought one hand to her face and gently kissed her, trying to tell her all he felt without words. How much he admired her. How holding her in his arms made him feel at home for the first time in his life.

He placed his hand on her waist and pulled her closer. Helen stood on tiptoes and gripped the lapels of his coat as they kissed more fervently.

The door at the top of the stairs slammed open, flooding them with light. Both Nathaniel and Helen shielded their eyes.

David called down to them. "Seems as if you two have worked out your problems. Time to come upstairs into the light."

"David," Cassandra called from behind him. "Let them

have some privacy."

"I'm looking after the concerns of my sister," David called back.

"Yes, please go back upstairs," Helen admonished him. She stepped away from Nathaniel but kept one hand in his. "You're being silly."

"Am I? Do you mind telling me what you're doing down here?"

"I'm certain you don't wish to speak of the many stolen kisses we shared before you married me," Cassandra remonstrated.

"Do you intend to marry her?" David asked, turning back to the couple.

"David!" Helen protested, mortified. Nathaniel squeezed her hand.

"If she decides we'll suit."

David sniffed and folded his arms. "Very well—I'll agree to it."

Helen snorted. "You're not required to agree to anything. I'm of age."

"Not required by the law." David came the rest of the way down the stairs. "But I couldn't be so lucky as to gain a sister and then treat her carelessly."

"Oh, David. The best of brothers." Helen let go of Nathaniel's hand to hug David.

After a moment, David hustled them all upstairs. "Come on then, a courting couple must be supervised."

"I can't imagine how you'll behave when our daughter has suitors," Cassandra muttered.

David grinned. "Not to worry; we'll just have sons."

After a round of congratulations on the courtship and

David's freedom, Cassandra gently reminded David that he needed to bathe and pulled him out of the room.

Helen moved closer to Nathaniel on the couch. "Are you certain you wish to entangle yourself further with this family?"

He dropped a kiss on her lips before wrapping an arm around her. "I've never been more certain of anything."

Epilogue

Temperance Hayes looked out over the dancers in her drawing room and pressed a hand to her hurting heart. This should have been her wedding feast.

Not that she begrudged her cousin her new seafaring husband. He was handsome enough, in his way, though clearly David should have spent more time teaching him to dance. At least Captain Carter had allowed David to convince him to wear something other than his stodgy black homespun. At least Captain Carter had allowed David to convince him to wear something other than his stodgy black homespun.

Blue suited Helen better as well.

The couple left the dance floor and joined David and Cassandra. In Temperance's opinion, no woman that great with child should appear in public. She had looked forward to her own children, but she would have been humiliated to go out like that—even for one of her own sisters.

Temperance watched as someone approached the bride and groom with slices of cake. They shared a look she could not decipher, and then Helen took the first bite of her cake.

She leaned forward when Captain Carter raised a fist to

Helen. He pretended to thump her on the back, and her cousin burst out laughing.

He could not mean to strike her at their own wedding feast. Temperance hoped her cousin had chosen better than that. Winthrop would not have behaved so.

"Enjoying the feast, Temperance?" David asked, suddenly appearing by her side.

Her stomach clenched, but she couldn't edge away from him. "Not really."

She ignored his expression of mild surprise. "Would you care to dance, then?"

"Dance with your wife."

"I have been, but she's tired now and asked me to make sure her cousins were engaged."

Temperance sucked in a breath. Thanks to him, she never would be.

"Shall I ask again?"

Her anger finally ignited, Temperance glared at him for three long seconds as the piece came to an end and the dancers applauded the musicians. In the brief space of silence between dances, she raised her voice to be heard. "You murdered Winthrop Morley."

The silence stretched out as it seemed half the room turned to them.

David didn't look away from her, though surely he was aware of the gazes upon them. Somehow, he kept his expression as indifferent and aristocratic as ever. "An 'I don't mean to dance tonight' would have sufficed."

After a moment, he nodded to the musicians, who struck up a cotillion. Slowly, the dancers took to the floor, and attention turned away from them.

David stepped closer to Temperance, turning his back on the dance floor and the closest would-be eavesdroppers. Now his voice did carry an edge. "I'll thank you not to ruin your cousin's wedding feast."

"Oh? You ruined mine."

"I would be heartily surprised if Winthrop intended to marry you."

Temperance glowered at him. She could march right upstairs and fetch the letters in Winthrop's hand to the contrary. He'd only been dead two months, and everyone else was dancing as if on his grave.

"I'll remind you the magistrate ruled it was clearly self-defense, not murder," David continued. "I never intended—"

"The magistrate trying curry favor with you and your father? That one?"

Clearly her cousin-in-law's temper was wearing thin. "He had a pistol, Temperance. I wonder which of your cousins' husbands you would have preferred to have died that night."

"Better you than him, Lord David."

She hadn't used his courtesy title in years, and judging by his flinch, her words had hit their mark.

"Apparently you haven't noticed," Temperance began, turning to fully face him, "but smuggling is illegal."

"And punishable by instant death? At the hand of the governor's son?"

"According to you two."

Lord David answered with only a single syllable laugh, as if that fact were a mere inconvenience. She supposed it was, when one was rich and noble.

"Get out of my house," Temperance muttered.

He forced on a smile. "I'm hosting this feast."

"Well, I cannot stand to be in the presence of a murderer a moment longer." She stalked from the room.

"Have some cake!" Lord David called after her, as if their conversation had been nothing more than typical party fare.

The feast occupied the whole of the dining room as well, so Temperance marched right out the front door.

It took all of two minutes on the walk in front of the house to wish she'd had a better plan. A January night in Philadelphia was hardly the place for a fine gown. She had been too angry to pause for a cloak.

She began pacing, rubbing her arms. How long did she mean to stay out here? Surely Lord and Lady David would be among the last to leave.

She should go back inside and straight upstairs, but Lord David would certainly see her.

She could never forgive him for what he'd done. Never. Even if everyone in the city seemed content to pretend Winthrop had never existed and Lord David Beaufort was some conquering hero.

Temperance turned back toward the door again and spotted a man approaching. She tried to gauge how quickly she could make it to the door, in the event this man bore some ill will.

He stopped at their stairs, and Temperance halted. She shrank back into the shadows, hoping he wouldn't notice her.

At the steps, the man kicked snow off his shoes. He was almost to the door when he glanced in her direction—and then quickly looked back. "Temperance? Is that you?"

She peered through the shadows at him. "Step into the light?"

He backed up a few paces to the light from the windows.

"Owen Randolph?" Her voice shook with the cold. She'd

hardly seen him since they were children. What was he doing here?

"How do you do?"

"Cold."

"Oh, ah." Owen glanced around, then quickly shrugged out of his great coat. "Here."

She allowed him to place the coat around her. For a moment, Owen's arms draped around her shoulders, and she remembered how it felt to stand wrapped in his comfort. When they were small children, they were the brightest lights in one another's worlds.

Worlds that were made dim by being abjectly poor. She pulled away from Owen, tucking his coat's warmth tight around herself. "What are you doing here?"

"Oh, your father and your . . . cousin? He said I could come. David?"

She scowled. "He's only married to my cousin."

"I see."

Temperance tried mightily but couldn't conjure a reason why Owen Randolph might have wangled an invitation from either of those people. "How did they come to invite you?"

"Ah, at the office. They said I should come?"

Naturally her father would be at his workplace, and Lord David lived in the flat above the law office. But that didn't explain Owen's presence. "And what were you doing there?"

"I'm studying law. From your father?"

Was he asking her? "How long have you done that?"

Owen squinted at her. "Two years."

How had she not known this? And how had Owen managed that? Last she'd heard, he'd been a stable boy.

"Do you mean to go in?" Owen asked.

"No." Her tone brooked no argument.

Owen hesitated. "Perhaps you should, though? Quite cold. That coat won't be enough for long."

Temperance glanced around. "Can you make sure he doesn't see me?"

"Who?"

"Lord David," she practically spat.

"Your cousin?" He quickly added, "In-law?"

"Yes."

Owen was clearly mystified but acquiesced. He motioned for her to approach but didn't move to the door. "Come," he said, his voice gentle. "You're frozen."

Temperance stepped closer and allowed Owen to touch her, rubbing his hands over her arms to warm her. She looked up into his blue eyes. There had been a time where they shared everything, the closest of friends.

Owen met her eyes and stilled. He swallowed audibly.

"Thank you," she said, only a whisper.

"Anything for you."

Temperance remembered herself and stepped back. She gestured at the door and Owen took her meaning. He opened it and ushered her in.

In one surprisingly deft move, Owen lifted the coat from her shoulders, used it to conceal her until she was on the stairs, and whirled away.

Temperance paused before she disappeared to go find her letters again, craning her neck for one last glimpse before she was out of sight.

Owen Randolph had grown up.

Dear Reader,

Thank you so much for reading *A Lady to Lead*! I'm excited to share my first sweet historical romance with you. I hope you'll continue to join us for all romance of the Revolution!

Do you know the best way to thank an author when you enjoy a book? We do love getting notes from happy readers, but even more helpful is leaving a review online on Amazon or Goodreads. Reviews also help writers get advertising spots and spread the word about a book.

Until my next book comes out, I'd like to invite you to join my mailing group! I've got lots of fun bonuses there, including tart recipes, smuggling facts, that corner chair (it's a Chippendale!) and more! Join me here: http://love.didavisauthor.com/newsletter2

Thanks again for reading, and I hope to see you again soon!

Love,

Audrey Glenn

Acknowledgements

Thanks to my family for all the awesome suggestions!

Thank you to Ashlee, Jessica, Amanda, Allison and Sally for helping improve this book.

Thanks to my coconspirator Diana Davis for investing so much of your time and for talking me through it.

About the Author

*A*udrey Glenn is a voracious reader who has long loved historical romance. She's a big fan of the classics—*Pride and Prejudice, Jane Eyre, North and South*, to name a few. She loves studying little-known stories of American history and holds a degree in political science. She lives in North Carolina with her husband and kids in a perpetual fixer-upper.

Made in the USA
Columbia, SC
04 December 2021

50448021R00135